A MESSAGE FROM BATANG

A MESSAGE FROM BATANG

Owing to the antiquity and rarity of this book, certain pages are regrettably absent, and readability is compromised due to the blurring of the original text. If you possess any insights regarding the availability of these missing sections, kindly inform us. Your assistance is crucial in ensuring the completion of this significant work for the benefit of future generations.

A MESSAGE FROM BATANG

Z. S. LOFTIS

Published by

FacsiMile Publisher
12 Pragati Market
Ashok Vihar, Ph-2
Delhi - 110052, India
Phone: 011-47034999
Email: www.facsimilepublishers.com
info@facsimilepublishers.com

Distribution Network
gyanbooks.com
India, USA, Canada, UK, Australia

ISBN: **9789332892446** (HB)
First Published, 1911

2nd Impression 2025

Printed at: Gyan Press, Delhi.

A MESSAGE FROM BATANG
Author: Z. S. LOFTIS

A MESSAGE FROM BATANG

A MESSAGE FROM BATANG

The Diary Of Z. S. Loftis, M.D., Missionary To Tibetans

Z. S. Loftis

A MESSAGE FROM BATANG

Z. S. Loftis

ISBN : 9789332892446

First Published 1911, reprint 2013 in India by

Isha Books
B-69, New Gupta Colony,
New DDA Market, New Delhi - 110009

Printed at : Sagar Color Scan, New Delhi.

The City of Batang

To his Mother
and
the cause he loved

"You take the Bible to the heathen and he may spit upon it, or throw it aside as worthless or harmful. You preach the Gospel to him, and he may regard you as a hireling who makes preaching a trade. He may meet your arguments with sophistry, your appeals with a sneer. You educate him and he may turn from a heathen to an infidel. But heal his bodily ailments in the name of Christ, and you are sure at least that he will love you and bless you, and all that you say will have to him a meaning and a power not conveyed by other lips."

DR. GEORGE E. POST.

Syria.

Preface

THE task of writing this preface has seemed most difficult; not the work, but that I may use the words he would wish me to use, that what I write may reach the hearts he hoped to reach, that out of his labor and his thoughts may come the power he would wish them to have.

Whatever was difficult, whatever was tiresome, whatever trials he had on his long journey, he made no complaint in his little book, and it could not have been all easy.

The knowledge he gained that no one before him had hitherto acquired, especially concerning the great Litang Monastery, has the right to be given to the world through his name.

On seeing the solitary grave three days out from Batang, if then the tragedy of his fate entered his soul, we can never know; but if it did he came off victor from the struggle, and bowed his head in submission to the Higher Will, and we are the losers. His ability, his knowledge is lost, such a loss I could never make you know or feel.

> "So many worlds, so much to do.
> So little done, such things to be;
> How know I what had need of thee,
> For thou wert strong as thou wert true.

Preface

"The fame is quenched that I foresaw,
The head hath missed an earthly wreath;
I curse not nature, no, nor death;
For nothing is that errs from law.

"So here shall silence guard thy fame
But somewhere out of human view,
Whate'er thy hands are set to do
Is wrought with tumult of acclaim."

—*Tennyson.*

Batang, West China.

Autobiography

Z. S. LOFTIS, M. D., was a native of Tennessee, born in Gainsboro, May 11, 1881, where he lived until he was seven years of age. His parents then moved to a Kansas farm, where he worked during the summer and attended school during the winter months. After several years the family moved to Central Texas, where his school work still continued. During spare times he learned the printers' trade and studied photography. He became a Christian at the age of thirteen and was actively identified in Sunday-school and church work. Upon the death of his father in 1898, he was thrown largely upon his own resources. In 1899 he entered the Department of Pharmacy in Vanderbilt University from which he graduated in 1901, winning the Founders' medal given to the honor man of the class. For several years he worked at retail drug business and in manufacturing laboratories supporting his mother.

It was while doing slum mission work and teaching in a Chinese Sunday-school in St. Louis that he felt a call to become a medical missionary. He then offered himself to God for that purpose and set about trying to secure a medical education. He came to Nashville and entered Vanderbilt Medical Department, working outside school hours each day to earn money to pay his expenses. In the summer of 1906 he was sent by the college to the Southern Students' Y. M. C. A. Conference at Asheville, North Carolina. As yet he had not decided on any particular place, but was praying that he might be sent to the most difficult and needy field in all the world. At the Asheville Conference he heard of Tibet. The very fact that it was a closed land and so difficult of access caused him to pray that he might be sent there. During his senior year in college he served as president of the Nashville Student Volunteer Union. In January, 1908, he was appointed by the Foreign Christian Missionary Society of Cincinnati as a medical missionary to Tibet. Shortly afterwards the Vine Street Christian Church of Nashville pledged to support him as their representative in the foreign field since he was an active member of that church, being much interested in the Sunday-school and city mission work. Graduated from Vanderbilt Medical Department in June, 1908, and sailed for the foreign field, September 18th, the same year.

Contents

I.	Bound Towards the Orient . .	13
II.	Nearing the "Far East" . .	20
III.	First Glimpse of China—Shanghai	25
IV.	In and About Nankin . . .	31
V.	Up the Yangtse	42
VI.	On Towards Batang . . .	50
VII.	Overland Towards the Tibetan Border	64
VIII.	In the Tibetan Passes . . .	81
IX.	At the Top of the World . .	97
X.	Lodging in the "Forbidden City" .	109
XI.	The Journey from Litang . .	123
XII.	A Lonely Grave	135
XIII.	Above the Clouds	138
XIV.	Batang at Last	142

Illustrations

City of Batang . . . . . *Frontispiece*

On Board the good ship "Mongolier" *Facing page* 14

House for Chinese Soldiers near Shanghai . . 26

House-boat on the Yangtse River 26

Entrance to Ming Tomb at Nankin, China . 36

Chinese Arch 36

Gehwji near Samba 100

Dr. Loftis in the Coracli 100

Kanger Building 120

Principal Hall of the Litang Monastery . . 120

Mr. Soutter's Grave at Samba 136

Headman at Samba 136

Grave of Dr. Loftis at Batang 144

A Message From Batang

I

Bound Towards the Orient

S. S. "Mongolia," Sept. 15, 1909.

AUGUST 31st I left Nashville, Tenn., for Cincinnati, Ohio. The day was a very busy one, and at 8 P. M. my train was off. About fifty of my friends were at the depot to wish me good-bye, and during the last moments sang, " God be with you till we meet again," and repeated the Mizpah benediction. The memory of this will always be dear to me. As the train rolled away the long trip had really begun, and I was at last started on my journey.

Arriving at Cincinnati I remained the 1st, 2d and 3d for the annual Missionary Conference. There were about thirty-five old and new missionaries present, and we spent the time in a spiritual feast. September 6th found me at home in Rogers, Texas, where two of my cousins had arrived the day previous to wish me farewell, and so we were a happy bunch. We went to Sunday-school and church in my old home church. The next few days were spent very busily and happily with mother and my old friends. September 10th I bade mother and my other loved ones farewell, and started for the coast. Arriving in San Antonio I found my train late, so went to visit the Alamo. There I entered the rooms occupied by our brave men, and stood by the spots made sacred by the shed blood of those who gave their lives for the cause they loved. It made my heart swell with emotion as I thought of Bowie, Travis and Crockett, who were glad to serve their country thus. What a privilege to lay down one's life for a cause he loves.

On September 15th, at 1 P. M., the good ship *Mongolia* left her moorings, and the steady throbbing of the great engines began. I stood on deck and watched the waving mass of humanity on the pier, but knew no soul there. My last farewells had been spoken. We slowly steamed out through the harbor, through the Golden Gate and then the prow of the ship was pointed towards the southwest. There was no sorrow in my heart as I saw the loved native land fading in the distance, holding all that was dear to me except my work. I turned my face and heart towards the setting sun, and began to settle down for the long voyage.

September 17th.

I opened my first steamer letter to-day and it made me very happy to know how my Vine Street friends love me. It is quite inspiring to know that good true people are praying daily for me. How I wish they might know how well and happy I am to-day! The ocean is a glorious sight, almost as

On Board the Good Ship Mongolia

calm as a large river, the sun shines directly down, causing the water to glisten with the dancing light. I begin to be able to appreciate more and more the poems and stories of the ocean. Two expressions especially have been running in my mind, "Roll on! thou deep and dark blue ocean, roll," and "Spread round all, old ocean's gray and melancholy waste." The day closed with letter writing, and in reading "The Lady of the Decoration," laughing and crying over it.

September 20th.

The first Sunday on the ocean! How different from the last two! We had services after the Episcopal form, and the old familiar hymns sounded as good out here as they did at home.

September 21st.

Early this A. M. the ship was astir with subdued excitement. Passengers were out on deck at daybreak, eagerly looking for a glimpse of that beloved "terra firma" which had seemed so far away during part of the voyage. To the south could be seen a long, low, dark mass of color which we soon saw to be land. On the opposite side we could see large, rough rocky hills which we were told was the island on which Honolulu was located. Soon we were summoned to the dining-room, and found that we must be inspected before we could land. The steward came down with a bunch of letters which he began to distribute, and I for a moment felt a longing for a letter, when I remembered that all my mail would come the way I had come, and necessarily could not reach me here, but just then the steward handed me a letter addressed to my own self. A lady who had been similarly surprised a month before passed the delightful experience along to me. As we neared the pier some eight or ten native boys were seen swimming in the water, and diving for the coins which were cast into the sea by the passengers. They would watch the piece of money plunge into the water, then swim towards the spot where it disappeared, dive after it, and invariably catch it before it had reached the bottom and bring it up triumphantly. They kept it in their mouths for want of a better pocket, then called the admiring passengers to throw down more. We soon were ashore, but somehow I didn't feel at home on solid ground, and had difficulty in getting about with as much facility as usual. The ground didn't rock and sway like the ship, and my feet were surprised at the ground not coming up to meet them.

The first place we visited was the market house. There I saw many fruits I had never dreamed of, and many others whose names I had heard but had never seen. Fish of all kinds, sizes and colors, from tiny shrivelled ones that seemed to have been pulled before they were ripe, to the big ugly devil-fish. I left the market feeling that nature had indeed supplied these Hawaiians with plenty to eat, and was thankful I didn't have to taste at least a little of each new thing I saw. Next we caught a street-car, and travelled through a regular maze of beauty. Right here I pause before the immensity of the task before me!—that of describing what I saw. In order to do it justice I should have to kiss the Blarney stone several times, then for a pen, pluck a feather from the most gorgeous hued bird-of-paradise that ever lived; and for ink I would need a concentrated mixture of ten thousand selected rainbows, mixed with a few tons of the brightest tropical flowers, all dissolved in the most highly colored ocean in the world; while for a scroll I would need heaven's broad expanse, tinted with the combined beauty of a dozen of the most exquisitely colored sunsets which nature can paint.

All this and more would be needed to adequately convey the faintest conception of the beauties we saw. Nature must indeed have been in lavish mood when she poured out her cornucopia of beauties on this favored spot. There may be other spots more beautiful, but I'm from Missouri! Then we went out along the famous Waikiki beach, the finest in all the world; through the trees we caught sight of the ocean, and never did I dream that water could assume such delightful hues. The waves burst into milk-white spray, and came curling in on the clean white sand. Then beyond were the most delicate tints of green and blue, shading off into the sky so gradually that it was hard to tell where one began and the other ended. Next we visited the aquarium which is reckoned as the finest in the world. The fish were all on parade, as if conscious of their beauty and gorgeous coloring; even the ugly devil-fish did a few stunts for our special benefit, but it made one get white around the mouth, he got so angry when we tried to arouse him to activity. If it were possible for me to describe the fish I saw I wouldn't do it, for my friends would read my description, and sadly shake their heads, and say, "Poor boy! I feared it. I almost knew his mind would give way under the strain of leaving home and loved ones, and at last it has happened." We came back to town and out towards Diamond Head, through a lovely valley, with the most delightful homes we could possibly imagine. I think I would be satisfied if I got to heaven, and was shown a home as beautiful as some of those, and was told it was to be mine eternally. After a most delicious lunch at the Y. M. C. A. building we went across the street and saw the first frame building erected in the islands. It was built in 1821, having been shipped around the Horn, and was in the island a year before the king would allow it to be erected, saying, "No one should live in a finer house than he."

We then visited the Royal Palace, and saw the throne room, and a little of the splendor of the departed kings and queens of Hawaii. There was something pathetic about the beauty which seemed a mockery of the departed power of an extinct government and its rapidly disappearing people, as the race is being absorbed by the other nationalities which have invaded the islands.

Another car ride took us out into a beautiful valley, past the tombs of the kings and queens, "The powerful of earth," for even in this fairy-land people die. At present there are only two of the "royal line" living, and soon the last will have been laid in "their last resting-place by those who in their turn shall follow them," and so we get our lesson, "And yet a few days and thee the all-beholding sun shall see no more," and are reminded that we should live not as those who have no hope, but sustained and soothed by an unfaltering trust, approach our "grave like one who wraps the drapery of his couch about him and lies down to sleep and pleasant dreams." There is so much of beauty, so much of sentiment on these islands, that one feels that it is indeed fairy-land, where all the inhabitants are fairies, and every day a holiday.

As the ship left the harbor the divers again followed us, sporting in the water as if it were their native element. As the land once more faded in the distance, we turned our faces westward, while our hearts were filled with praise and thanksgiving to God for the joys of this day. The sunset was most beautiful, and I was loath to go indoors and leave nature for even a few hours.

II

Nearing the "Far East"

September 25th.

THERE was to have been a dance on board this evening, but owing to the death of a passenger it was postponed. An old gentleman and his wife were going to Japan to visit one of their children, but it will be a sad meeting that will occur when the poor old mother greets her child alone, and tells her sad story.

This has been the second death so far as I know that has occurred since we left San Francisco. The other poor man was buried at sea, and in the night time. Out of respect for the dead, the machinery was stopped, and the corpse, wrapped in its shroud, was dropped over the rail into the deep, cold sea. There was a splash, a ripple on the ocean's bosom, then the sea closed over the spot, and the body sank into the dark depths, "without a grave, unknelled, uncoffined and unknown." There were few to watch the sad burial, or to mingle their salt tears with the ocean's briny ones; but at that last great day when the trumpet shall sound, will not this man rise from his watery grave to stand before his King to be judged just the same as the man who was buried with pomp and glory in an expensive, hermetically sealed casket, where the worm and the water cannot enter? Yes, we shall meet him there when we, too, go to receive our reward.

September 29th.

To-day the wind was blowing a good, stiff gale, driving the rain and spray before it in blinding sheets. This, with the fog, made it impossible to see more than a short distance from the vessel. The wind shrieked and whistled through the shrouds; the captain anxiously walked the deck and bridge, looking for anything that might mean danger to us. The wind drove the spray like snow, taking it off from the surface of the water, and blowing it along in streaks, sometimes pitching it up and whirling it round and round, like dust in a whirlwind on a summer day. About noon the sun came through the clouds, and every wave that burst into spray had its rainbow. Every moment the picture would change: never the same. Every wave and every rainbow had a beauty all of its own. It was all gloriously different, so that one would never tire of the wonderful panorama of ocean views which the kind Creator so freely displayed for our enjoyment, it seemed. My heart swelled with gratitude and emotions unspeakable. I felt no fear, because I knew the Master was guiding us, and that He was just the same as when aroused by His frightened disciples during a storm, He calmed the angry tempest by "Peace be still," and the winds and waves obeyed Him. I knew the

Father held all this wild, turbulent, stormy ocean in the hollow of His hand, and not one of the agitated elements could harm me without His consent. It was great to feel that my Father controlled all this, and that it was all His. Some of the old familiar songs took on a deeper meaning after what I had seen. For example

"Jesus Saviour, pilot me,
Over life's tempestuous sea.
Unknown waves before me roll,
Hiding rock and treacherous shoal."

This can only mean more to one who has seen the unknown waves rolling before him as far as eye could reach. "Lead kindly Light amid the encircling gloom," comes with greater force when you see the fog settling down around you, and hear the shrill blast of the wind and roar of the waves about you. It is worth while to be able to look up into heaven and know that your Father is on His throne, and nothing can go wrong.

October 2d.

When I arose this morning I looked out and saw land again, the first view of the "Sunrise Kingdom." Soon after landing we found ourselves seated in jinrikishas, and headed for a restaurant. This was something new. Here I was in a little one-seated, two-wheeled buggy, with a man for a horse. I thought the proper name would be "Pull-man car." He trotted up streets and down streets, and finally reached our destination where, amid many profuse bows, we went up-stairs to a large table, and after great exertion succeeded in ordering dinner. After sightseeing for some time we came back to the wharf, and finding a launch, started for the ship; ran aground trying to get out of the harbor, spent an hour getting off, but finally reached the steamer in safety.

October 5th.

Found us passing through the famous Inland Sea; beautiful islands were all about us; and the blue water still and smooth, with its many sails, small fishing craft, and here and there a coasting vessel puffing out black smoke, made a pretty picture. After I have heard the missionaries speak in Japanese to the people, I have been most anxious to get down to the study of my language, so I can work with my people, the Tibetans. How I long for the time when I may tell of Him who sent me to minister unto them, using their own language!

October 6th.

When I awoke we were in the harbor at Nagasaki, said to be the best protected harbor on the globe. This is the second fastest coaling station in the world, the record being 4,000 tons in nineteen hours, all done by hand! There were about fifty coal barges around the ship. Ladders were quickly built up against the sides, and the human chain was formed. Men and women on the barges quickly filled the small grass baskets, and they were started up the line. They moved as steadily as if by machinery. All day long they would keep this up, receiving about forty cents a day.

October 7th.

Out in the Yellow Sea! The last day on the ocean. To-morrow I reach the land which henceforth is to be my home. I begin a new life to-morrow. The same person, but a new life. I leave America behind when I leave the *Mongolia.* May God help me to be worthy of the charge. To-night I went out on the prow and enjoyed the beauty of the sea. The moon was almost a cloud, flooding the sea with silver. When it would disappear I could see the phosphorescence in the water to better advantage. It was very bright, and the ship seemed plowing through a sea of fire. The ship has now anchored off the bar waiting for morning. I feel happy to know that to-morrow will mark a new era in my life. I leave old friends and scenes, and enter upon an entirely new field of work. May God bless my efforts, and help me to be humble and prayerful.

III

First Glimpse of China—Shanghai

October 8th.

DISCOVERED China to-day. Woke up and saw land in the distance. Looked at the water and found it as muddy as it could be. The great Yangste here empties its load of sand and silt into the sea, and pushes it out for fifty miles into the ocean. We started up the mouth of the Yangste, which here is fifty or sixty miles across. We soon dropped anchor, and as I came down the steps I bade farewell to the dear old *Mongolia*, which was the last tie between me and America. It was a long way to the wharf, but at last our launch arrived, and two of our missionaries were there, and gave me a hearty welcome and some letters. I had a letter from the Batang people giving me so much desired information, and making my heart glad to know they were so thoughtful of me.

Well, here I was in China at last, the day I had dreamed of for many long days; but it was no time for dreaming now. Our baggage attended to, we started for the missionary home. The streets were swarming with Chinese of all kinds, who would be most unattractive but for the fact that they possess a human soul which our Master loves.

In the afternoon I started out shopping, but first had some money changed, and if the Japanese coin is bad, this is terrible. I got a handful of different coins, no two of which were exactly alike, though some were of the same value. I was told that a dollar was worth more than ten ten-cent pieces, and several other paradoxical things. Started out along the street to see things, and, well I saw them—shops, tea-houses, travelling restaurants, old Chinamen and young ones, beggars holding up a stub of an arm or a sore hand. Once in a while a foreigner, and semi-occasionally an American face. Here I was chasing around on the streets of Shanghai, China, alone as I would in America. The great trouble was I couldn't "rubber," badly as I wanted to, for the minute I began to look around I showed that I was a tenderfoot, and a half dozen "rikisha" coolies would spot me, and swarm around to make me ride. My only chance was to look absolutely unconcerned, and strike out down the street as if I knew just where I was going and why, and then they would let me alone.

Only one member of the *Mongolia* passenger list besides myself is here, and I feel that indeed the crowd is scattering. To-night I'm writing these words alone, in a little room at the very top of the building (for it's mission money I am spending, and I must not be hard to satisfy); my observation today has told me that there is an immense amount of work to be done here in Shanghai, and furthermore that it will take a long time to do it with all

House for Chinese Soldiers near Shanghai

Houseboat on the Yangtse River

the counteracting evil forces foreigners are importing.

October 10th.

I went around to see our school in Shanghai, and saw a number of bright-faced boys studying with all their might, and out loud, too. It made me very happy to see them, and the good work here. They gave me a Chinese name, Lo E Sen (Dr. Lo). A most cordial invitation was extended to me to come and work in Nantungchow, and I couldn't help but feel the strength of the appeal. A great field, money already provided for the hospital, two nice homes already built, and enough work to keep half a dozen busy for a hundred years! Such an opportunity! How I wish I had another life to invest there.

I went to our mission here for Sunday-school and church. There was quite a number present, and some had such good faces; men I could not help but love and trust. One good old elder impressed me very much, as well as an old Bible woman who had spent thirty years in the Master's service. At the close we had a very sweet communion service with the Master, and I left much happier for what I had seen.

In the afternoon we had another very delightful service, and I was introduced and spoke a few words. As there were a number of children present I thought of my own Vine Street Sunday-school scholars, and the interesting faces I looked into a few Sundays ago in Nashville, as I told them good-bye. Then I told the Chinese children of the Vine Street Sunday-school, and how they had sent greetings and love to them. I saw their faces light up with interest as the interpreter spoke, and they all stood and desired that I send their love and greeting to my little friends in America.

Another thing I did before the morning service was to go with Mr. Ware to some tea-shops with some leaflets. He told me to say "Please look" in Chinese, and so I passed out a number with these words. They were all received very kindly and willingly, some were read and some carried away.

I was very happy to do this, my first service for my Master here in China. May God bless the seed thus sown, and may it bring fruit to His honor and glory.

At nine o'clock in the evening went to another service held by Chinese boys who have to work during the day, and therefore have to meet at this time. They have a room rented, and defray all expenses themselves. A very earnest and consecrated set of Christian boys. It was an inspiration to look into their faces. When they were told where I was going they were much interested, and asked many questions, and one suggested they have a word of prayer for my safety on my way. So we stood with bowed heads while one of these boys carried their petition to our Father's throne that I might have a successful and safe journey. As I heard my new name presented to the Father by these my Chinese brothers, my eyes filled with tears, and even now as I write my heart swells within me as I think of these consecrated Chinese Christians, doing this loving service for the Master's servant. Those few moments alone more than repaid me for many weary hours of trial I have had to reach this place. May God shower His blessings on this band of noble boys. It has been a glorious day, for which I am very thankful.

October 13th.

Started for Nankin to-day. Boarded the train at twelve o'clock, and was soon going through the country. Little farms were all about and people watering them. The canals form a fine waterway system. We passed a number of villages where the people lived in little grass huts. One thing that impressed me very much was the immense number of graves everywhere to be seen. Thousands and thousands of graves dotted the fields as far as the eye could reach, and scarcely at any time could I look from the car window without seeing these countless mounds. As I mused on the multitudes that slumbered here, the horrible thought flashed over me that these were all graves of heathen, of men and women who had gone down to the grave without the knowledge of Jesus, and without hope. What a scene it will be when, on the last great day, they shall stand before the judgment bar and say, "We did not know—they, your disciples, did not tell us."

The train reached Nankin in the evening, and I was greeted most heartily by our missionaries there, visited the hospital, and saw what an immense work is carried on here, enough to keep one-half dozen men busy at home.

IV

In and About Nankin

October 17th.

EARLY this A. M. a Mr. Yang, a Chinese evangelist who had been in Ta chien lu, called to see me, and gave me some valuable information concerning the work there, and method of travel, also much of the danger of the trip, and I realize God must guide my frail little boat through the rapids.

In the afternoon an outing had been planned for the newcomers. We were to go to the Ming tombs about five miles from the city. On the way we made several stops, one in an old temple where we were shown the footprints of holy blood. The story is that a Chinese emperor was about to be slain, and his prime minister sprang between him and danger, and was killed. His "blood stains" are still shown on the table, yet the temple is hundreds of years old. We went on out the east gate, left our rickishas and started on foot for the tombs. Our road led through what seemed to be an immense graveyard; thousands of graves were about us, many were dome or bell-shaped, marking Buddhist tombs. Many others were simply made by placing the coffin on the ground, and covering with a bit of earth. Often the coffin was bare, the soil having been washed off, or rooted away by hogs.

We walked for a mile or more through these graves to reach the "Avenue of animals." This road led to the tombs, and was built four hundred or five hundred years ago. On either side of the road are great stone statues, representing various animals as well as men, some standing and some crouching as if to spring. Always a pair of animals of the same kind, one on either side of the avenue facing each other. There were lions, tigers, camels, elephants, men and horses. Many had been carved from a single stone, pedestal and all, and some of them weighed tons, since they were larger than life size, several more than fifteen feet in height. On many were heaped a great number of small stones, which had been thrown by natives who believed that if they threw a pebble up and it remained, the prayer which they had just made would be answered. We went on across some massive piles of masonry which had once been the gateway to the enclosure within which, somewhere, was buried the Emperor Ming, founder of the Ming Dynasty, which flourished before Columbus crossed the Atlantic in his little ships.

We passed through two or three large gates, and past great tablets supported by immense stone turtles, past slabs of stone sunk in the ground upon which were carved fantastic and grotesque figures of the Chinese dragon. Everything was on such a massive scale that the very size of arches and carvings was wonderful, and must have represented the slow, patient labor of untold thousands of poor heathen. Grass and trees had grown up all about and within the walls, the stones were moss covered, and worn with ages of rain and snow. It was here we got a most magnificent view. The sunlight was sifting through the clouds in long silvery rays, touching in the distance the broad surface of the Yangste, making it glow like a ribbon of burnished silver. Then the city of Nankin enclosed in its great stone wall which stood out sombre and cold with its serrated top like great teeth. Next the broad plain strewn with the tens of thousands of grassy mounds and rough coffins where slept those who had helped build all these magnificent arches and palaces. The stone animals stood like great silent sentinels guarding the post, while just at our feet lay the crumbling walls, and within were the walks and gardens, long since bereft of the busy throng, for many centuries fallen asleep. After returning home we sang a few of the old songs, and it was a little hard to realize this was China, though when we sang, "Way down upon the Suwannee River, far, far away," there was a peculiar accent on the words "far, far" which I had never noticed before.

October 18th.

Went to a communion service in the morning, and afternoon went for a stroll and walked about among the graves, as there is no place else to go, and came back through some narrow streets filled with odors! The Chinese don't seem to know what a sewer is, so everything that is waste is thrown into the streets. Great green slimy pools are very plentiful, and seem to contain the filth of centuries, and I guess they do. Hog-pens are often built adjoining the house, the object being to save building but three sides to the enclosure, a brilliant idea! Sometimes for safety and convenience the hog is kept in the house.

October 20th.

Went with Dr. Macklin on a preaching tour into the country, seven or eight miles from the hospital building. We travelled through some very beautiful farming country, through green fields and pretty roads, past little hamlets half hidden among trees. Passed a number of small temples, and looking in could see the hideous idols, and it almost made my "flesh crawl" to think that people were actually worshipping these things. Finally we reached a little village, and stopped at a tea-house. We seated ourselves on a little bench at a dirty table, and a dirty old woman served us some tea in some very dirty cups, from a very dirty teakettle. The bowls were sterilized with boiling water, and as the tea was made from boiled water, we were comparatively safe from cholera and like germs.

We were no sooner seated than the doctor began to talk and preach to those about him. The tea-house with its contents and inmates was a study. The building itself was made of bamboo, mud and straw, the inside was almost black from the smoke of ages. In one corner sat an old woman spinning a kind of linen thread. There were a half dozen small tables around, where Chinamen were sitting and drinking tea, smoking and talking. A barber was plying his trade near by on a bench, shaving his customer's head with a peculiar little razor having a broad but short blade. Some men stood about looking on. A few women with their babies were sitting about watching us. Some larger children played about on the floor, which was only hard earth. While the doctor was preaching a little baby about two years old was brought to us. It had a very bright face, but when we looked into its eyes we saw it was stone blind in both, and that the little hands that groped slowly about its father's neck were in darkness that would never more be lifted. All caused by neglect and ignorance, coupled with sin. It made me sick at heart as I thought of the doomed future before it, of being a beggar in the midst of spiritual darkness even greater than the physical.

October 26th.

I still study in the hospital, and to-day witnessed rather a gruesome sight. One of the patients died yesterday. He was put in a vacant room, where he remained alone till this afternoon, when his friends came for him bringing a rough, unlined, unpainted, wooden coffin. The coffins are pretty well made, of heavy timber four or five inches thick, and well joined. The body was placed in the coffin with no bathing, or other preparation, in the same clothes in which he died, and with wide-open, staring eyes, the lid fastened on, and all borne away by coolies to be buried.

October 28th.

Visited a Taoist temple. A priest kindly showed us through the building and we saw where incense was burning to gods of wood and stone. My heart was heavy within me as I saw an intelligent man prostrating himself before the idols who had eyes but cannot see, and ears but heard not.

November 5th.

Heard a very strange superstition to-day connected with the manufacture of vermicelli in the city of Nankin. For some reason Nankin is supposed to be a very unstable city, after the fashion of a boat,—a boat's sails being up makes it more easily upset by the wind. The vermicelli in process of manufacture is hung up to dry, and thus resembles sheets or sails. This is apt to bring about a sinking or upsetting of the city. So the officials have a ruling prohibiting the making of vermicelli within the walls. Therefore it is made, and has been for centuries, across the river. Near the city is a cave in which is a stone boat chained to the cave wall by a huge iron chain, and so long as this chain remains unbroken it is dangerous to make vermicelli in the city. In the boat lives a great snake which prevents any one from breaking the

Entrance to Ming Tombs at Mankin, China

Chinese Arch

chain, or removing the spell. Recently, however, some few Chinamen have been venturesome enough to risk disaster, and are making the article within the city, though perhaps without the knowledge of the officials. So we may look for some terrible calamity! The fact that such superstitions are dying out is a favorable sign, and indicates the approach of the time when China will throw off the shackles of superstition and ignorance. God speed the day when she shall be a Christian nation!

November 30th.

"Johnny" has arrived and soon came around to see me; he is a smiling, happy Chinaman, and I am sure will take good care of me on my Western trip.

Went with some of the older missionaries on an itinerating trip, and while our boat was anchored, we got out for a walk and heard most pitiful crying, and we proceeded to find the cause of the disturbance, which proved to be an opium suicide. A man had swallowed one-half dram of opium, and he was fast becoming unconscious. We went in and started to work. Gave the fellow a dose of apo-morphine and strychnine, and waited results. The man was unconscious now, but we began the fight against death, resolved to cheat him of his victim, even if only for a short time. With a wet towel we slapped his back until he began to be aroused, and soon he began to vomit. However the fight was not yet over. Enough had been absorbed to cause death, so we began walking him up and down the floor, and jerking him about. It was hard work, but after a time he was awakened enough to say, "Oh, I'm so sick," and I didn't doubt it a bit; apo-morphine has a habit of making one sick. When the old mother and wife saw that life was coming back, they came and fell at my feet, their eyes full of tears, and profuse thanks on their lips. We lifted them up and went on with the battle, but I can never forget the gratitude of those poor people. I felt extremely thankful for this opportunity to do a little service for the Master.

December 15th.

"Johnny" paid a visit, anxious to know when we can leave. I am as anxious as he is, but can't hurry as my freight has not yet arrived from Shanghai.

December 25th.

Such a beautiful day outside, and a good day to be happy. I spent the morning quietly thinking of the Christmases past, and trying to remember them. I remember the place and time of each one, even '86, '87, '88 and '89, which were spent in Tennessee as a little child remembers them, and thus in God's mercy I have had many pleasant days spent in many places, and to-day I am under a Chinese sky, 10,000 miles away from kindred and the home ties, but as near God as never before, and one year nearer my heavenly home than ever before.

December 31st.

The last day in the old year. The sun has set the last time for me this year. Alone I sit in my room to-night, thinking of the past year, its joys and sorrows. I have been on my highest mountain peaks, and in the deepest shadows of my life, but the mountain peaks are far greater in number than the shadows. There have been sorrows, such as I hope I shall never see again, and there have been opportunities I fear I shall never see again. I bow my head to the dying year, and bid it a final farewell; it will always stand out as one of the greatest for me. I thank the heavenly Father for His love and care, and for all the year has brought me, and pray that it has not been lived in vain.

January 1, 1909.

Greeting to the New Year! So another milepost has been reached. I find myself starting a new year indeed, new scenes, new people, new language, at least to me it is all new, yet "old as the hills."

February 18th.

One afternoon I spent a pleasant time climbing the three highest peaks of Purple Mountain. The highest rises 1,450 feet above the city of Nankin. The mountain has much legendary and historic interest, and is much loved by the Chinese. It was occupied by the rebel troops during the Taiping Rebellion, and later by the Imperial troops. On one of the peaks, an old fort in ruins is found, and a marvellous system of breastworks and fortifications, extending for miles out into the surrounding country, connecting many smaller hills. A splendid bird's-eye view is obtained from the top, showing the situation to have been well-nigh impregnable.

Many dozens of smaller villages and hamlets are to be seen in the valleys, while the thousands of graves stand out prominently. Many of the private cemeteries being interestingly laid out, and approached by avenues of stone men, horses, camels, turtles of immense size, all reminding you of a past that must have been gorgeous with its oriental splendor in the centuries that are gone. In the evening a telegram came saying my freight was coming, being five months on the way. Everything arrived in good shape, so Johnny and I got busy packing. Johnny is a brick, and is giving me splendid assistance in getting things ready. Sent a telegram to Batang, stating we would start the 20th.

February 20th.

In the cold gray of the dawn I arose, folded up my bed and got ready to travel. Soon the boat was ready to leave, and as it moved slowly away I waved a last farewell to my friends, and saw the city wall with its great gates and Purple Mountain in the distance growing dim. I knew the long four months' journey into a far country had begun in earnest. This then was no longer anticipation but realization. It is really hard to realize I am off for such a journey, but I am indeed happy, and very grateful to God for this day. Taking a last glance at the familiar, templed hills that somehow had grown strangely dear to me, I went to my cabin, and turning to Exodus xxxiii. 15 read, "If Thy presence go not with me, carry us not up hence." Then to Proverbs iii. 6 and read, "Acknowledge the Lord in all thy ways; He will direct thy paths." Then my favorite Psalm cxxi., and then the ninety-first which had only last night been sent as a parting message. Then on my knees I asked the Father to lead and direct my footsteps, and so I place my hand in His for Him to lead me where He wishes, remembering my Saviour's promise, "Lo, I am with you always."

V

Up the Yangtse

March 3d.

Ichang at last! One thousand miles up the Yangste!

March 5th.

As my house-boat went alongside the wharf this morning, I went down and had my things put on board, and stored away in the hold where they will have a chance to get wet. The nights here are interesting. There is a group of Chinese huts just below my rooms in the city, and they make a lot of noise with drums and gongs all night to keep the devils off, I suppose; any self-respecting devil would keep away from such noise, so I sleep with my window open without fear.

March 7th.

This is the day for the "March Offering" for foreign missions at home, and I am hoping and praying that it may be a good day with them.

March 9th.

At 4:30 P. M. we moved apart from the other boats, and started slowly up stream. The long river journey had begun at last. I must confess I felt more like I was starting on a long journey into a "far country" than I had before. While I didn't feel like a "goner" I do have a kind of "gone" feeling. My cook prepared me a good supper, and I ate to my full capacity. We are now anchored up the river a few li above Ichang. The two younger sons of the captain are about as dirty specimens of kidhood as I have ever seen. They have taken a special liking to me. I gave one a piece of candy, and since then I have been deluged with Chinese candy, and they get around me while I read and write, rub against me until I'm going to have to make a demonstration in self-defense, I fear. There are two now pushing their dirty noses in my face, and rubbing dirt off on my bed and clothes.

March 11th.

The first thing to do to-day was to go up a small rapid, at least Johnny said it was small, but as it was my first, it looked like a pretty big one. I stayed on board, however, and enjoyed it hugely. The boat tossed about like an egg-shell over the rapids and waves, but slowly and surely we crept up inch by inch until we were safely over. There were wrecks of several boats lying about, and I can hear the roar of the large rapids through which we are to pass to-morrow. It is the terror of all going up and coming down, and many boats get smashed to pieces here. But I do not fear the result, for the boat is in the hands of a Higher Power than the captain's, and if He wants to lead me safely through He can do so, and I know that He knows all, and will not let anything happen that is not for the best. Good-night — "Be Thou with me always."

March 12th.

By one o'clock our boat had begun to get ready to go, and I determined to stay on board while we ascended the rapids, as I knew I could get an idea of them to be obtained in no better way, and I rather enjoy an element of danger. We were lying in the edge of a great whirlpool, which drove our boats up towards the rapids with great force. The boats tossed and strained, and the bamboo cables cracked as if they would snap to pieces. The current from above was forcing the boat ahead of me down, and the whirlpool was driving mine up stream. That boat was older than mine, and somewhat rotten and in a few minutes I saw we were in danger of colliding. Two of the large cross-beams hooked together like the hubs of passing wagons, and in a moment the one on his boat cracked and broke like a match, splintering the side very much. So Johnny and I, to prevent further damage, took our stand at the windows, and with our hands pushed heroically. That we helped some there is no doubt, but for some time the boat was in great danger.

Our turn came next to ascend the rapid. We were tossing about like a chip, and the roar of the waters was deafening. It was almost impossible to stand, and everything that could fall off of anything had been taken down and placed on the floor or bed. There could be no doubt that the "Sintan" was a terror. As I looked at the roaring, dashing, settling torrent, I knew that a boat uncontrolled could not live in it, much less a man. The waves were four or five feet high. The water at this point flows at the rate of fourteen or fifteen knots an hour. It is almost a waterfall. The descent is so great for a few feet, that standing as I did almost on a level with the water I could see how much higher it was above. For a short distance the fall must have been ten feet in one hundred yards; a very great fall indeed. Four huge bamboo cables were fastened to our boat, and about one hundred coolies were pulling. Following them inch by inch we advanced, our progress being almost imperceptible. In ten or fifteen minutes we had scarcely advanced so many feet. The men pulling strained every nerve and muscle, while those on board used the sweep and rudder with marvellous dexterity, keeping the boat off the rocks. The sensation one gets from such an ascent as this for the first time is certainly a new one. I am not a stranger to artificial thrills such as looping the loop, shooting the shoots, the Ferris wheel, etc., but none of them offers the sensation one gets here. Take the suspense thrill of the "Loop the loop" when you are sitting head downward and prolong it for twenty or thirty minutes, and you get some idea of what this is like.

All is fairly quiet to-night, except the roaring of

the rapids we have just passed. The heavenly Father has protected me through another day of danger, and to Him I give thanks and praise.

March 17th.

St. Patrick's day. Well, I suppose at this very minute the people at home are gathering on the street for the parade. St. Patrick's day is an innovation the Chinese have not yet adopted. We passed through the wind-box "gorge" early this morning, while it was scarcely light, but I got a fine glimpse of its magnificence. About the only narrow escape I had to-day was the breaking of a window in my face by a bamboo pole, which got away from a boatman and sprang back and broke the glass.

March 19th.

To-night we are anchored within the influence of the "New Dragon Rapid." The motion of the boat is something more than usual, and the roar of the rapid is very distinct. This is a new rapid, caused by the sliding in of a part of a hill a few years ago. A freighting company wanted to blast it out and clean the river, but the Chinese would not consent, saying that if the spirits wanted the rocks to fall in the river, it would displease them to have them removed.

March 27th.

In trying to cross the stream, the swift current threw us against a bank with considerable force, and it looked as if we would be upset, but it was a sandy bank, and we only got a little shaking. All seemed to be going well, it was just dark, the men were looking for a place to stop, when suddenly we struck a rock and stuck fast. The men got out and began to try to get the boat off. It began to move after a bit, when all at once there was a crash and a sound of inrushing water. Pandemonium broke loose. Well, there was something doing for the next several minutes. Partitions were torn down, tables, chairs and boxes hustled out of the way. Things hurriedly taken out of the apartment where the leak was; some of the men carried things out on the front deck while others frantically dipped out the water, and sought the hole. Rags, cotton, etc., were brought, and the aperture plugged, the boat was pulled to the shore and propped up to keep it from upsetting if it sank. We were told to get our things and get off. I felt about the least excited of any, and quietly got some of my most valuable things together where they could be easily secured, and waited for developments. It was eleven o'clock before they ceased working at the boat. Things were piled around in a reckless manner, and the ends of the room all open to the night. However it gradually became quiet, and we breathed normally again. So I am thankful to the heavenly Father for His care. To Him be all the praise, honor and glory for all good things, and thanks to the Master for His promise, "Lo, I am with you always."

mountains which have been in sight for two or three days. I watched the twilight settle down, and wished it were possible for me to photograph the scene as it was, in all its varying colors, from the delicate tint of a few wild roses, to the sombre colors of the great red cliff and its shadows.

April 28th.

About noon we saw some artificial caves cut in the face of the cliff. The openings were set back under a kind of stone portico and decorated with crude carvings. I was told they were the dwelling places of a wild aboriginal race that existed many years ago. How long ago, and all the strange story of these vanished people, no one can tell. To-day I caught sight of a large saddle-backed mountain and with my glasses saw large drifts of snow lying in the most sheltered parts of it. Upon inquiring I was told that it was Omei Shan, one of China's famous mountains made so by its many Buddhist temples, and the pilgrimages made by thousands of devout Buddhists every year.

I wonder if this is really the last night on the river? The captain is counting on getting to Kiating to-morrow afternoon. So if we do I am enjoying the last quiet night on the house-boat. As we travelled along to-day we passed a big cliff with a hole of peculiar, natural formation in it. I noticed the men who were now rowing had brought a lot of small stones, and as we neared of the day in contrast to the darkness through which we have been passing. The most delightful thing was the Christian fellowship. I had scarcely realized the weight which the night of heathenism had fastened to my heart until I came once more into touch with His followers, and realized the contrast. That there is a devil in China is a fact that to my mind needs no proof. The day has strengthened and helped me much, for which I give thanks unto the Giver of all good and perfect gifts.

April 6th.

Johnny and I crossed the river this morning, and went to work repacking the medicines for Batang. Found them in a terrible condition, bottles broken, medicine spilled and instruments rusted, but repacked them as best we could.

April 7th.

Made an early start by opening a lot of boxes and found a lot of blisters on my hands as the result. I got busy repacking again, and "Trying to hustle the East"—all my urging seems to have little effect on the Chinese carpenters and tinsmiths whom I had at work. Too busy and dirty to eat I worked away. The slow tinners were terribly exasperating, and when I wasn't at work I paced the floor and pulled my hair. Finally about five o'clock the last case was packed, and I sent them all across the river to the boat. So a hustling day was over, and a good deal accomplished towards getting away.

VI

On Towards Batang

April 9th.

When I awoke this morning we were already under way, and slowly leaving Chungking behind us as we had left Ichang, one month ago to-day. About ten o'clock we reached the customs barrier, got my papers signed without delay, and am O. K. for Batang now.

April 11th.

Easter Sunday, so I've been told, for I'm sure I don't know whether it is or not.

April 14th.

The captain got so mad at the trackers to-day that he came near having a fit. He let off some of his fury by throwing a tub of cooked rice into the river, but nothing serious happened. The twilight period is delightful now. It is unusually long after the sun disappears behind the hills before darkness falls. Then I enjoy sitting out on the front of the boat and inhaling the fragrance from the opening leaves and buds of the many trees which cluster about the cliffs and rocky places on the hills. The many colors suggest autumn rather than spring. The farmhouses in the distance, nestling among the trees, look quite homelike, and I can almost imagine myself back in the homeland again, and feel like listening for the tinkle of the cow-bell, as of old. A few mosquitoes have been buzzing about for the last few nights but they seem not to have seen a white man before, and scarcely know how to treat me. I can't say that I care to cultivate their acquaintance too much.

April 19th.

We were progressing fairly well this morning when we ran aground, and stuck hard and fast on a long, flat stretch of sand and mud. The boatmen first tried to get the boat off with poles; that wouldn't work, so a number of the traders were called in and helped push and shove. In about fifty minutes we were off and proceeded on our way. One of the boatmen fell overboard, backwards, just as we were crossing a small rapid, but was quickly rescued by another. He was so badly scared that I couldn't keep from laughing, and haven't got through yet. I have seen several fellows fall in the river and get pulled out, and every one seems so badly frightened that he doesn't know who he is.

April 20th.

It is two months ago last night since I left Nankin to begin this trip. And two months ago just at daybreak saw the old city walls grow dim in the distance. I have been following the windings of the Yangtse ever since, and am now about 1,800 miles up the great river. One old fellow has been too sick to talk for a couple of days, so he has been lying about grunting. I have diagnosed his case as malaria, and am loading him up with quinine, in the hope that I may make a demonstration of the power of foreign medicine.

April 21st.

After dressing this morning I opened the door and found my patient sitting up, picking off lice, and I knew without asking that he was better. This is the first time I have met with such a symptom, but I soon learned its value. After we had anchored for the night a number of suspicious, disreputable-looking fellows came down, and inquired rather carefully about us. The captain decided they were planning to rob us, and were getting the lay of the land. So he came to Johnny and implored that I fire off my guns, and let them know we had foreign firearms. So I got out my revolver and Winchester, and fired a few shots from each into the water, then reloaded and continued reading the story of the tragic ending of Mary Queen of Scots. Everything is quiet yet, and it is 11 P. M., and dark as a "stack of black cats." Just at this moment a sudden noise brought Johnny and the cook to their feet in eager expectancy, but it proved a false alarm. As for me I shall retire as usual, and "lay me down in peace to sleep." The Lord forgets not His promises.

April 22d.

Almost before I realized it we were in sight of Sui Fu. I made ready to go ashore as soon as possible, and it was not long until we turned up the Min River, and left the bosom of the Yangste which had carried us so long and so far. It was with just a little bit of regret that I said good-bye to the great river. For nearly 2,000 miles I have traversed its length amidst dangers, and over its smooth surfaces when it was as quiet as our own Mississippi at its best. Though many times it has been like a roaring lion seeking to devour us, yet it has been my friend in the end, and it is the last unbroken tie that binds me with the homeland, for it flows direct to the great ocean that kisses the sands of loved America, many thousands of miles away.

April 24th.

We started up a small rapid to-day, and I thought the size of the rope looked rather tiny, so I was not in the least surprised when just as we were about through to smooth water it parted, and we drifted back even further than we had come the day before. It was enough to make a fellow feel like swearing, but I compromised by going to bed and remaining an hour trying to forget I was in a hurry. This travelling on the Yangste (but we are on the Min now) may be hard on the nerves, but it is decidedly harder on a fellow's imagination. He has to imagine all sorts of things. That he is not in a hurry at all, that he doesn't care if he does lose a day or two. He must imagine he is travelling at a high rate of speed, when he may take sight on some stone or tree on the bank and find half an hour later that he has moved six feet and seven inches up stream (if he is so fortunate as not to have drifted back a mile or so). He must imagine the captain is doing his level best to hurry on, and all delays and accidents are unavoidable. He must imagine that he has an unlimited supply of patience, and that he doesn't care a rap whether he gets to the end of his journey this year or next. All this is quite a strain, and unless his imagination is decidedly well developed, he is apt to have trouble and suffer from necrosis of the funny bone before he has finished his travels. Well, Flanigan wired: "Off agin, on agin, gone agin;" we make another start with a new rope, and in an hour or so are safe above the rapid. It is evening, and we are tied up with a lot of other boats at the foot of a big cliff and all is quiet at 10 P. M.

April 25th.

This morning one of the captain's children brought me a bunch of wild roses. They were rich with perfume, and only simple pink blossoms, but I cannot remember when flowers seemed so sweet. I placed them on my table, where they have shed fragrance and sweet memories all day. Little did the poor little dirty heathen child think how much they were prized by me. I have put in the day reading the entire book of Acts and making an outline especially of Paul's travels. I found it a splendid thing to do, and it has shown up the brave old missionary in a clearer light than I have ever seen before, and I admired more than ever the man who braved the dangers unflinchingly for the sake of the Master, "whose he was and whom he served." My prayer is that I may imbibe more of the spirit of this grand apostle, and prove as steadfast and loyal as he did, even though I cannot do the great work that he accomplished.

April 26th.

This evening the captain halted, saying he was unable to go beyond a rapid just above until morning, so I went out to look about, as it seemed to be a picturesque spot. It is just in the bend of the river and the boat has been drawn up amidst and against some huge boulders, and made fast with great bamboo cables. Just above us towers a perpendicular cliff of a brick-red sandstone, hundreds of feet in height. On its top and round about are a number of tall slender pines, already being trimmed for masts for Chinese boats. A few grass-covered huts are built at the foot of the cliff, while a short distance up the river is a heathen temple, with its queer roof and peculiar architecture. A few scattered patches of wheat, peas, etc., finish this side of the picture. Across the river in the distance is a range of rugged peaked mountains which have been in sight for two or three days. I watched the twilight settle down, and wished it were possible for me to photograph the scene as it was, in all its varying colors, from the delicate tint of a few wild roses, to the sombre colors of the great red cliff and its shadows.

April 28th.

About noon we saw some artificial caves cut in the face of the cliff. The openings were set back under a kind of stone portico and decorated with crude carvings. I was told they were the dwelling places of a wild aboriginal race that existed many years ago. How long ago, and all the strange story of these vanished people, no one can tell. To-day I caught sight of a large saddle-backed mountain and with my glasses saw large drifts of snow lying in the most sheltered parts of it. Upon inquiring I was told that it was Omei Shan, one of China's famous mountains made so by its many Buddhist temples, and the pilgrimages made by thousands of devout Buddhists every year.

I wonder if this is really the last night on the river? The captain is counting on getting to Kiating to-morrow afternoon. So if we do I am enjoying the last quiet night on the house-boat. As we travelled along to-day we passed a big cliff with a hole of peculiar, natural formation in it. I noticed the men who were now rowing had brought a lot of small stones, and as we neared the hole began to try to throw their rocks into it. It was nearly full of similar stones, and the sides of the cliff all beaten up by the many stones that had missed their intended destination. My curiosity was aroused, and inquiry brought out the superstition that if a man succeeds in landing a stone in the hole, his prayer for a son will be granted. If he fails his prayer remains unanswered.

April 30th.

As we neared Kiating one striking thing I saw was a giant Buddha cut in the solid stone. The face of a cliff had been cut with the likeness of a Buddha, now with trees for its hair and shrubs for eyebrows. It is rather a remarkable piece of work, and is quite commanding and evidently very, very old. This is my first night to be spent in a house for nearly two months, but somehow it seems natural again. So this part of the trip has been made safely, and I am thankful for the many blessings and manifestations of God's love to me on this part of the long journey.

May 3d.

Started from here in a three-bearer chair while Johnny and the cook had a two-bearer each. The men kept up a pretty good pace, and rapidly covered the ground. I soon got used to the motion of the chair, and amused myself by looking around to see what was going on. I found plenty to interest me. First the rice fields. They were in a variety of stages, some were being plowed by men and the water buffalo, both wading through deep, muddy water. Others were setting out the rice in bunches a few inches apart. Some were pumping water into the fields from irrigation ditches, using a peculiar endless-chain pump, only paddles instead of cups were used. Besides the rice crops I saw corn, wheat, oats, peas and beans, and tea. After dinner we jogged along the "big road" which was about two feet wide, paved with large slabs of soft stone, and led in and out around and between the fields, often on top of a small ridge, with a flooded rice field on either side, where a misstep might have meant disaster. We passed a number of old, artificial caves cut in the cliffs, and I went in to examine some of them. There was a large room high enough in which to stand upright, while at either side were benches hewn out of the walls a few feet from the ground, used evidently for beds, while smaller recesses were for the reception of small articles, I suppose. The caves were damp and dark and gave one an uncanny feeling. They gave but little trace of being inhabited at present, except occasionally by coolies as a refuge in time of a storm. In one I saw a few broken pieces of pottery, and an ulna and a few vertebræ. Perhaps these places were the first dwellings of the men who were ancestors to the present Tibetans, and as the Chinese civilization pushed them farther and farther westward, they finally died out and disappeared altogether in this part of the country, leaving only those caves their only homes.

May 4th.

At noon we stopped at an inn, which was practically the same as the street, and had dinner. A crowd of gaping, staring Chinese stood about watching the "foreign devil" eat, tearing his food with "knives and forks." A fellow soon gets to be the centre of attraction out here. He is followed about the street as if he were a whole circus parade, and they stare at him as if he were a three-headed calf, a man-eating gorilla, or some other freak. As usual there are many graves with peculiar stones. There have been many arches, temples and shrines all now in a state of rapid deterioration.

About 8 P. M. it began to drizzle. The chair men put on their umbrella-like hats, and also fastened a small metal shoe to their straw sandals, not unlike a small donkey's shoe, to prevent slipping on the wet stones. Stopped at a Chinese inn. I was given the best room, and found it better than out in the rain. It is back at the end of the house, overhanging the river which at present flows a few feet away. It is perhaps twelve feet square. Two windows, or rather two sections of the wall, open out on the river, giving plenty of much needed air, for when I came in I could scarcely see for the smoke which came from the kitchen fire just in front. The furniture consists of four verminous beds, covered with straw or matting, a bench, and a table of boards in one corner. The floor is dirty, the walls black with smoke. Finding a flight of stairs running down beneath my room, I went down to investigate what might be below me. I found one of those inevitable foul smelling pits of human refuse. It is three feet by six feet and several feet deep, filled with an abominable rotten mess which is literally alive with maggots, and gives an odor which is suggestive of anything but balmy breezes and Arabian perfumes. The cook prepared a good supper for me, which I ate on a table in the next room, a few feet away from a urinal, which was in a near-by corner, and in use while I ate. Nevertheless I enjoyed my supper very much. My cot is opened up on the top of one of those filthy beds, and I will trust that the bugs do not climb the legs, and get to me to-night.

May 5th.

After a day's travel of climbing my first hills and through valleys of bamboo, crossing and re-crossing rivers, it was rapidly getting dark, and I had no idea where we were when we stopped at a little bunch of houses; the cook said we were at Yachow. I was surprised indeed. However I told him to find a foreigner, and pretty soon I found myself in front of a large foreign building, and upon knocking, was met by the doctor in charge, who gave me a hearty welcome, and ushered me in, saying I was to stay there. A nice supper was prepared, which

I heartily enjoyed, as well as the company of the doctor and his wife.

May 6th.

As it was still a few days before my freight could come from Kiating by raft, we had to do something to help pass the time, so a trip to the country was planned. We started for a city forty miles away on foot. It rained, and we got rather wet, but our goods finally came in good condition, and we made ourselves at home in a foreign preaching place, and were comfortable, and could write and pass the time quietly until ready to return.

May 7th.

Spent part of the morning writing, and then went out to look around the city. One of the first things we ran across was a Chinese theatre. The stage as usual faced the temple, and the audience stood in the open court. The scenes or play represented some historical event in ancient times. The costumes were sometimes quite gorgeous, and always exceedingly grotesque. Some of the acting was quite good. There were comedians, tragedians and others of various parts and talents. These plays often last for days. There was quite a crowd, and we stood for some time watching a fellow near us scratching off smallpox scabs, but it didn't seem to disturb any one. One counter attraction was a pickpocket being "spanked" on the hands with a rough board. Later we saw a number of fellows being punished. Some were fastened up in cages, with their necks between great planks. Others had a great board about two feet square fastened around their necks, so that it was impossible to get the hands to the face, or lie down.

May 10th.

Returned to Yachow yesterday. This morning we spent the time about the hospital, reading and writing. The rafts having not yet come, there was little that we could do towards getting on with our journey. Spent the evening talking until about 10 P. M. A pleasant, quiet homelike day.

May 11th.

My birthday. However I said nothing about it to any one, so passed the day without special demonstration. In the afternoon several of us visited a place where the tea is compressed into a kind of brick for shipping to Tibet. The tea leaves are first steamed, then packed into a mold and turned out on a long flattened cylinder weighing about eighteen catties. These are wrapped in bamboo matting. The tea coolies sometimes carry as many as four of these bales over the mountains to Ta chien lu. The tea is of poor quality to begin with, and mixed with a lot of sticks and leaves. The water used is most filthy looking. So the chances are that the tea must contain millions of germs. In the evening met Dr. Laufer of the Field Institute, Chicago. He is bound for Tibet in the interests of anthropology and ethnology.

May 15th.

My goods arrived this evening, all dry and in good condition. Had five thousand pounds in all. Arrangements were made to get away early on Monday. So by night we had things pretty well under way for our start on the morrow.

May 16th.

About noon a man came in saying he wanted me to go and see a girl that had taken opium. We gave her the usual vigorous treatment of apomorphine and strong tea, and walking her about, and with a small electric battery succeeded admirably in keeping her awake. By 3 P. M. we were able to leave her and go home to dinner. When we returned she was about straightened out.

VII

Overland Towards the Tibetan Border

May 17th.

WE were up by daybreak this morning, and began to get ready to get away. After breakfast we took leave of our kind hostess, and the other friends in Yachow. They had treated us most delightfully, and we enjoyed our week with them to the utmost. The most of my freight was left to follow by coolies later, while I took only a few of the most necessary things. I walked a good deal. We saw coolies carrying a lot of medicines, among which was a splendid quality of licorice. We met three French travellers, and stopped to talk with them. Met load after load of the wax insect which is carried by coolies from a point about twenty days from here. The insect is put on the mulberry tree, where they excrete or secrete a fine quality of white wax. Another most interesting thing was some big wooden slabs being carried by men and horses. They are called "scented boards" by the Chinese. The odor is very pleasant. They are mined from the earth like coal. They are practically indestructible, being a kind of lignite now, and are very expensive, and used for coffins. Stopped in a very good inn, but it is late and we are sleepy. Will stop for the day.

May 18th.

We passed a mountain almost covered with tea shrubs to-day. This is quite a tea centre. The hill-sides are steep, but mostly cultivated. We crossed a bridge built of huge stone slabs, the largest I have ever seen anywhere. How they were placed across the stream is about as much of a problem as how the stones for the pyramids of Egypt were put in place. The scenery was most interesting, and I delighted in it.

May 19th.

It is three months to-night since leaving Nankin on this westward journey, and the end is not yet. This morning the road began at once to ascend into the mountains. We followed the course of a small roaring torrent; most of the way it was a succession of cataracts, just enough to keep the stream milk white most of the time. We had a long climb of twenty or thirty li to the top of the pass, ascending about 6,000 feet in this distance. The view was most glorious as we ascended until near the top. The ravines and mountainsides were covered with a jungle so dense that it would have been impossible to get through without cutting a path. Many plants were familiar, but most were new to me. Bamboo predominated, at first a few feet high, but as we ascended it grew smaller and scrubbier until it was little more than coarse grass. Vines, ferns, moss, weeds, flowers and shrubs covered the ground, until in the distance the mountains seemed covered with green velvet. There were dozens of new and beautiful flowers on all sides, gradually diminishing as we climbed higher. There were many large trees lower down, but as we neared the top they grew shabby and gnarled. About half-way up cultivation ceases. The highest crop is corn, small and yellow. Many trees had the most beautiful foliage I have ever seen. The leaves were as vari-colored as in autumn at home, except all the colors were found on one tree. There were reds, greens, yellows, and some almost black, with all shades between. This made a beautiful picture indeed.

It was a perfect day, almost ideal for crossing a pass, and we could see clear to the tops of the mountains high above us. It was all so magnificent, I could have shouted for pleasure at the view. As we journeyed upward we passed many poor coolies with great loads of tea, coal, salt, etc., some loads weighing two hundred or three hundred pounds. As we got higher it grew colder until we were quite cold. Some snow and ice were near us, but none on the pass. It was the highest I had ever been, and I wondered if I would be affected by the altitude of 9,600 feet. But although I walked I felt no more inconvenience than the same exertion would produce at a lower level. Perhaps not so much, since the mountain air was in a way stimulating to me. We reached the top about 1:30 P. M., and had a wonderful view of range after range of mountains on both sides. Some must have been 14,000 to 15,000 feet high, and had some snow on them. We had a hearty meal of "oil tea" at a little rest house. The stuff is a kind of oily mess made of corn-meal, etc. Hogs were drinking swill in the rooms; some were stretched under the table asleep. Dogs, chickens and cats ran about under our feet, eating and getting in our way. But by this time I have gotten used to such things, so that they do not bother me in the least, and I eat with as much relish as ever. We rapidly descended until we reached the city about 4 P. M. It is quite cool and pleasant and we should sleep well.

May 20th.

We left the city and crossed a deep ravine, and then up a steep mountainside, though not more than 7,500 or 8,000 feet. The road was not so good as yesterday, being narrow and rough. The most striking feature of the country to-day was the bareness of the mountains. They were almost void of vegetation. The soil was a very poor, brown, rocky soil. The mountainsides were worn with great ravines, so as to almost ruin them for cultivation. This seems to be a peculiarly dry belt, in which there is little rainfall except at certain seasons of the year, and then it pours in such quantities as to wash mountains and roads terribly. The mountains to-day have been hidden largely by clouds and fogs, so that we could see but few high ones. Some, however, appear quite stern and forbidding.

May 21st.

The morning dawned with a clear sky, only a few banks of clouds hovering over the tops of the mountains. We started out on foot, and followed up alongside a magnificent gorge a thousand feet deep in many places. The scenery was very picturesque. Vegetation became more in evidence as we advanced into a damper belt. The air was clear, and as we went up the mountainside the view grew more and more beautiful. Houses showed a different style of architecture. In one place we saw the ruins of Tibetan buildings. We stopped for dinner at a dirty inn, where we had some coarse corn cakes and eggs. This ascent was more difficult to me than the other, the road being very rough, and quite steep, but the actual climb is only about 3,000 feet. About 2:30 P. M. we reached the top, which is about 9,500 feet in height. The road almost at once began to descend. Here we saw a Tibetan idol, and a proclamation in Tibetan. This spot has been, and is still supposed to be the dividing line of China proper, and the Tributary Country of the Tusas or kings of Tibet. The view from this pass was most glorious. The long valley lay behind us, between ranges of mountains, 10,000 to 11,000 feet high, their tops hidden in the clouds. About sundown we went outside the little inn, and saw that the clouds had lifted from the range, displaying them, more beautiful than ever with their covering of eternal snow. Beyond this range we could see the top of another peak, which is said to be about 26,000 feet. It was a sight new and beautiful to me, and I drank in the beauty of the scene quite eagerly.

May 22d.

The men had us up by daylight this morning, and once more we were on our way. The big snow mountains looked very beautiful in the morning sunlight, with the wreaths of white clouds about their summits. We descended into a long deep valley, and presently struck the Tong River, which we followed the rest of the day. The road ran around the edge of a cliff most of the afternoon; while riding along some one hundred or one hundred and fifty feet above the river, the chair bumped against a rock and came near tipping over. It isn't likely I would have fallen into the river, but it wouldn't have been a pleasant spill. I recognized two of my Texas friends to-day—the "Jimson Weed" and the Texas cain or prickly pear. The latter is said to grow nowhere else in the world but Texas, and it is a mystery how it got here!

I started out to count the tea coolies to-day. In two hours I counted fifty-two, but some were in the inns, so that I did not see all of them. I saw one fellow carrying two hundred and eighty catties, or three hundred and seventy pounds. Some women had one hundred and one hundred and fifty catties, while I saw boys twelve and fourteen years (maybe younger) with fifty to one hundred catties. This is the most cruelly hard work I have ever seen men do. The passes are terrible for them, and they may die on the road. The poor fellows only get about three hundred cash or fifteen cents a day for their work.

To-night we are in Lutingchow. We found the most disreputable inns that one could imagine. Rooms into which the sunlight has not entered since they were built. So dark you could scarcely see, dirty and foul beyond belief. We searched diligently for a better one, but in vain. We then tried a temple with better success. The priest took us in, and we have the whole temple to ourselves. I am now writing in the main room which is large, and has a good concrete floor. A few feet away is a table with incense and candles in front of a number of fierce-looking gods, and also some ancestral tablets. Just opposite us is a suspension bridge across the Tong River. It is built of huge iron chains fastened with stone pillars. The bridge is about six feet wide and three hundred feet long. It swings so when crossing, it is hard to walk without holding on to something. The floor is made of loose boards which have wide places, through which one could easily thrust a foot. But altogether it is a clever piece of work, and required some skill in the building of it. The chains are thirteen in number. Four chains at the sides form a kind of railing as it were.. It was a splendid idea, but like most Chinese architecture it was not carried out in its finer details. An iron tablet we found in a little hut after some search told the story of its erection. It was planned by a Chinese general in a Tibetan campaign of two hundred years ago. The tablet was erected in the forty-fifth year of Kang Hsi, what would be 1707 A. D.

The most interesting event of the day was a visit to a Tibetan Tusa, or king, in a small village a short distance away. He himself came and met us, and with much polite formality we were ushered into the guest room. We were not very suitably attired to meet his excellency, but he appeared not to notice the week's beard on our faces, and our travel-stained clothes. We saw a pleasant faced young man who lives in an ordinary Chinese house, wears Chinese clothes and queue, and speaks good Chinese in a low, pleasant voice. In spite of his Chinese surroundings it was easy to see he was not pure Chinese by any means. He talked to us of his subjects, and the families, and the way he governed, and of his tribute to the Chinese government. We now tried to bid our friend good-bye, but no, we must drink some more tea. Finally we insisted that our caravan was being delayed because of our stay, and so excused ourselves from remaining to dinner, which he urged us to do. However, our distinguished friend determined to treat us royally, and presented us with a large measure of fine rice and a large, fat fowl. He personally escorted us to the outer gate of his grounds, and so with a profuse exchanging of polite bows and good wishes we bade him good-bye. After a good brisk walk in the hot sun we overtook our boys, and the coolies to whom we exhibited our trophies, and entertained them with an account of our visit to the Tibetan king.

May 23d.

We first crossed the chain bridge, and continued along the bank of the river. As it was very hot, I did not feel like exposing myself to the sun, so I felt obliged to ride most of the time. But the dizzy height, and the sudden lurches of the chair made me cringe more than once, and voluntarily lean towards the face of the great cliff in which our path was cut. To make matters worse a strong wind blew vigorously as we crept around the sharp corners of cliffs hundreds of feet about the river. I found it easier to be satisfied with my position while reading, instead of staring out on the jagged rocks a thousand feet below. We passed many Tibetan villages and houses, while we saw an increasing number of Tibetan people. We passed one of their shrines with many prayer wheels and idols, where the devout Tibetan gives the drumful of written words a spin and thus offers up millions of prayers at one time.

At an inn we found one poor tea coolie who had fallen down with his load. In falling a big bit of corn cake had dropped from the top of his load, and struck him edgewise in the eye. The poor fellow was in great pain. On examination I found the sclera conjunctiva badly contused and swollen. I fixed up a little medicine, as best I could, to relieve and help him. Later in the day we passed a poor leper beggar woman on the roadside, on a high lonely cliff. At first the object seemed to be a shapeless bundle of rags on the rocks, but on investigation showed the hideous features of a leper. I shuddered as I thought of the terrible life of this miserable outcast, an exile from home and friends with begging as the only chance of warding off the death which is soon to come to her. Oh! for the Master's touch!

Soon the road led us around the cliff through much large cacti, down into a valley directly below us. The house we are now in is, if possible, worse than the one we escaped last night. Only one window, through which the sunlight cannot come. Walls black with smoke and dirt of years. Foul-smelling pools in front and behind. To-morrow we start on the final climb to Ta chien lu. We are virtually at a flight of stairs which lead to the roof of the world; not until I return this way again will I be below 8,000 feet. So I bid farewell to the lowlands again, and plunge into the mountain fastnesses of my people, the Tibetans.

May 24th.

We got a fairly early start and were soon climbing up towards the great plateau. Our road ran along the Ta chien lu River. This is a most wild mountain stream. It is virtually a continuous series of waterfalls all along the way. Its roar at times is deafening, and it throws spray many feet into the air and out on to the road. In many places it is crossed by a bamboo bridge made of a single bamboo cable strung with rings and a rope. Along this a passenger slides himself, one arm over the cable and one free to pull himself as he sits or hangs in one of the rings. We passed up a valley that was remarkable in many ways. The sides of the mountains were almost perpendicular in many places, the peaks rising to a height of 15,000 to 20,000 feet. There were signs of immense land-slides. Huge granite boulders dotted the valley. Beautiful waterfalls tumbled down the sides of the mountains from dizzy heights. I walked a good deal and got very lame. A rain-storm came up, and we took refuge beneath some overhanging rocks. Later in the day it turned cold and I was chilly with my overcoat on. We saw coolies carrying great loads of deer horns to be used as medicine. One woman was carrying a huge load of wood, and a basket in which was a baby about one month old. Another coolie carried a large fat hog, which was on top of his basket, and lay without a squeal or struggle, seemingly enjoying the ride. The mountains grew more rugged and wild looking as we went on, so that I became more and more fascinated with the country. Met many Tibetans, who are most interesting to me.

About 4 P. M., we ascended a slight rise, and thus below us lay the famous city of Ta chien lu. Long had I dreamed of this city, and I could scarcely restrain myself from shouting with joy at the sight of it. Its architecture is too interesting and complicated to try to describe now. I leave it for another day. We proceeded to the best inn, but found it occupied by our friend Dr. Laufer whom we met at Yachow. We had to go to another inn not so good, but it was the best we could do. The event of the evening was getting my mail. I sent Johnny to the office, and he came back with a coolie carrying a sack full of it. There were letters and cards by the dozens, an arm load of newspapers and packages. I started in on the letters, but only got through with a few to-night. The joy of getting a lot of letters after doing without one for over three months must be experienced to be appreciated.

May 28th.

After dinner we went for a walk to the wonderful hot springs here in the city of Ta chien lu. The water is so saturated with lime salts, that it has built up a bed some twelve feet high and several feet long, and a few feet wide. The water flows off in a solid stone gutter of its own making. When we returned a fellow came to me with a very bad finger. The end had been cut off, leaving the bone sticking through. I amputated part of the finger. It was done under cocaine with no pain to the poor fellow, much to his great astonishment and pleasure. He was blindfolded during the operation and great was his amazement when I placed the end of his finger in his hand. Later in the day we went for a walk through the city and beyond it. This is a most interesting place. The city is situated in a very narrow valley, with high mountains on three sides. They are covered with snow to about 10,000 feet. The city is not quite 9,000 feet above sea level. The buildings are mostly in Tibetan style, and are of rough stone rectangular in shape, and huddled together in Chinese fashion. The shops are full of interesting things both Chinese and Tibetan. The streets are full of lamas, yak drivers with their caravans, horses and animals of all kinds. We stopped at one place where some lamas were chanting prayers. They were seated on the floor, around a small low table on which were copies of their sacred writings. They would blow some brass trumpets a while, then ring some bells and beat on a drum, and then chant the prayers in a most weird voice. The whole thing was an interesting ceremony, and not without its musical qualities even if it was heathen. It was better than the Chinese noises which are disconnected, harsh and unmusical. Many mounds are to be seen all about the city. They are built up of slabs of stone on which are carved the famous "Omani padme hum." Prayer flags and mounds surround the hills, while everywhere we see them of paper and cloth waving in the wind.

May 26th.

Went out into the city to make a few purchases preparatory to getting away for Batang. After dinner walked out to the lamasery near the city.

It is a large, imposing place, composed of several buildings. We went into the outer court and halls of the large temple. It was very interesting with strange paintings covering the walls of the front portico or vestibule. We came out giving a big Tibetan dog a wide berth, and visited some smaller adjacent temples. Some were filled with the prayer drums or cylinders and flittering flags. Devout Tibetans passed around these cylinders giving them a whirl, thus offering millions of prayers in one second. In one building—I should not dignify it by the name of building, for it was a mere mud and stone hut—but in this was a huge cylinder about three feet in diameter, and six feet high, covered with leather, and with mystic characters in gilt on the outside. Inside it contained some half million or more written mani prayers. By means of a line and crank an old Tibetan was revolving it; at each revolution it rang a bell overhead, so that the number of revolutions could be the more easily counted. The old man was offering up prayers by the millions for the Tibetan women who wanted sons. They moved about the huge drum, bowing and prostrating themselves before it, from the four points of the compass. There was a wild look in their eyes as they went through this heathen ceremony. One of them dipped her fingers in the black lubricating oil on the axles of the cylinder, and smeared the tarry stuff on her face and neck. The sight of this ugly, hideous, dirty old Tibetan and the strange proceedings were things I cannot forget. It struck chill to my heart when I saw these deluded wretches groping so blindly in the dark for help from a higher power. I watched for a few minutes, and unable to stand it any longer turned away to hide the tears in my eyes, and went out with a great lump in my throat. May God help me to bring the light to these people, and to lay the burden of their souls' salvation on the hearts of the Christians at home! We went to another temple where hundreds of little lamps were burning before the idols, while lamas beat drums and chanted, whilst the devotees' lips kept constantly chewing the magic words "O mani padme hum" over and over. Sick at heart at the sight of all this, and the many obscene pictures on the walls, I returned to the inn to rest and read.

May 27th.

My cook "struck" to-day, absolutely refusing to go on with me to Batang. We argued the question every way, but nothing could persuade him not to leave me in the lurch. Chinese have been coming out from the mountains telling the most terrible stories about the passes, saying that arms, hands, feet and eyes have been freezing and dropping off. This seems to have him scared.

May 28th.

Began packing to-day in earnest, and everything was pretty well in order by the afternoon! Ula has been secured and we gave orders for the animals to be ready on Monday. The cook finally came round O. K.

May 29th.

The day dawned bright and clear. In the afternoon went out for a walk. The sun shone brightly most of the time. Large banks of fleecy, white clouds hovered around back of the mountains. The sky was a beautiful blue. The snow shone out in marked contrast to the great, dark rocks and cliffs of the mountain tops. Lower down their sides were green with vegetation. The city and river lay at their feet. The temperature was 69° Fahrenheit, yesterday 46° Fahrenheit. We visited two lamaseries. At one two fierce dogs acted as if they would tear us to pieces, but we kept our faces towards them, and managed to keep them off. We entered a large open court through a door near which were large "mani" cylinders. The lamas live in rooms around this court. The temple faced the gate of entrance. We ascended a flight of several stone steps to the outer hall, the walls of which were decorated with highly colored paintings of the wheel of life, Buddhas, the holy mountain, etc. A number of Tibetan men and women were prostrating themselves before these pictures and chanting prayers. Inside was a large rectangular room, with a dome in the centre. The side facing the door was occupied by various large, gilt idols and the sacred books; dozens of little lamps burned before the idols. The whole room was very dark, and you could see little by the dim light that came from the lamps through the open door. Two rows of drums and idols extended nearly across the width of the room. Around the walls sat devout lamas on rugs, turning prayer wheels, and droning out the everlasting prayers. Some kept bowing constantly to the gods, all dirty, lousy, and unkempt. Some of the furnishings of the temple were silver, a few of gold, and the rest brass and copper. Silken draperies and embroideries covered the walls, and hung from pillars and cross-beams, until the whole place seemed to be filled with them, mostly bright colored. From the dome hung long umbrella-like affairs of silken strips of cloth. They were of many bright colors, and formed as it were a huge tube or cylinder. The bits of silk were a few inches in width and length, and hung overlapping like shingles or scales. They were about three feet across, and some twenty feet long. A faint light streamed down from above somewhere within this mass of hangings, bringing out the bright hues of the silks. I could but tread softly in this place, so holy to the poor wretches, and pity their misguided worship. They certainly are the most religious people I have ever seen. If they would only serve God with as much energy as they serve their idols, what a difference it would make.

May 30th.

So this is the last night here in the inn. Tomorrow we tackle the passes. Now for the last grand, final rush for Batang.

VIII

In the Tibetan Passes

May 31st.

WE were up by daybreak, and glad to see that it was to be a clear day. Our "Ula" arrived early. Four horses for riding, and a lot of shaggy yak for the loads. Twelve animals in all. By 7 : 30 we had told our friends good-bye and were ready to be off. Reluctantly I left faithful Johnny behind to look after the rest of the freight which is to follow in a few weeks. We had an elegant day. We could hardly have wished for a better. There was not a cloud in the sky. As I rode out of Ta chien lu and reached higher ground, I got a view of the great, snow-capped mountains to the rear of the city. To our left rose a majestic range of mountains 20,000 feet in height, rough and jagged, but mostly covered with snow wherever it would stick. It was a magnificent sight we had, not a thing to obstruct the view. The air was sharp and clear, and the rough outlines of the peaks stood out against the blue sky as plainly as if it had been a picture. Each new turn of the road brought new scenes. The snow of the pass loomed up at times, reminding us of what was to come. Great granite boulders and cliffs lined the ravines, while at the bottom tumbles the roaring mountain stream. There were beautiful flowers everywhere, blue, white and yellow, which dotted the green grass like stars in the heavens. Rhododendrons of extreme size and beauty grew all over the mountains. Larch, pines and cedars were prominent among the trees. Gooseberry shrubs and scrub prickly oak were also much in evidence. Mosses, grasses and ferns filled the gorges with their beautiful verdure. There were few houses to be seen, but we passed and were passed by several caravans.

Mr. Sorensen of Ta chien lu, C. I. M., overtook us about 1 P. M. en route to Derge and thence to Chamdo. We came on together to Jeddo, where we stopped for the night in a Tibetan inn, or rest-house. There are a number of houses scattered about, which justifies the place having a name. It is also the end of the first day's journey. The inn is a dirty looking house of Tibetan style, built of stone and mud. We are all in a small dirty back room, the horses tied in the one next to us, which also does duty as a kitchen and general reception hall in the daytime. We stopped early, and I got a good view of the mountains as the clouds began to settle down on them. I went out and sat on a rock in the sun, watching them through my glasses. The snow and ice seemed to be from fifty to one hundred feet deep in places, and formed great hummocks. There seemed to be a few small glaciers far up on the sides. The actual elevation above the valley must be 10,000 to 13,000 feet.

My! but they are immense! Near by we found a hot spring, and had a good bath. It was quite a novel treat to lie soaking in a spring so hot that you could scarcely bear it, at an altitude of 11,000 feet, and watch the sun turning the snow on the mountain tops to beautiful colors of pink and gold in the evening sunset. It was a delightful bath in nature's own tub. One fellow there said his last bath had been taken last year. His looks confirmed the statement. The rest have all gone to bed, and I'm the only one up. From far below comes the faint roar of the stream. The tinkle of a horse bell can just be heard. The animals in the next room move about a little. A dog with bells on him scratched fleas to the accompaniment of their merry jingle, while a few mumbling words from some children give the human touch to the sounds. The first day en route to Batang. An interesting day, and not very tiresome either.

June 1st.

We at once began the ascent of the pass. It was somewhat cloudy, so that the view was not so good at first, but later it cleared up considerably. We followed the valley until about 8:30, when we stopped for breakfast. After eating we rode rapidly on, higher and higher until the few dwarf shrubs began to be small and few indeed. I had put on my overcoat as we were nearing the snow line. It began to be cooler, and though the sun necessitated a sun-hat, the coat was welcome. Soon we reached snow, which began to be more and more in evidence as we went up the mountain-side, until the ground was almost covered, and it was several feet deep at the roadside. Shortly before noon we reached the top; a magnificent view of snow-capped mountains lay behind us. Peaks covered with snow and ice were about on all sides, except just in front and to the rear. I tried to ride out on a little knoll to get a better view, but after the horse had floundered around in the deep snow a while, I gave it up and proceeded down the road. While crossing the pass we saw the remains of four yak that had died recently in trying to cross. This shows it is not all play. I felt no effect from the altitude, though the pass was 14,500 feet. We descended into a beautiful valley. The hills were not so rough and steep, and there was much good grass, and many herds of yak and sheep were seen grazing. We saw a number of black tents of the nomads. We stopped at 1 P. M. and waited for the boys. When they came they were scared nearly to death about the pass. My cook was almost panic-stricken, and had been all day. He feared all kinds of terrible things. This, with the altitude, gave him a headache and pulse of 128. I suppose he was sick. We went to see several Tibetan settlements, and quite a lot of land being cultivated. Wheat and barley were the chief crops, and it seemed to be rather a prosperous valley. We saw the remains of a strange stone tower; its original use is not known. It was evidently built some 2,000 years ago, and was 150 feet in height. Such towers are supposed to have been used either for defense, or religious purposes. About 5 P. M. we reached the little settlement of Nyang-Yanba, and hunted up the lamasery, where we found a good room. It is a stone building, typically Tibetan. We are on the third floor in the main hall, where the idols and holy books are kept. The walls are painted in flesh colors, and ornamented with lotus and other flowers. There are also a number of interesting scrolls which we examined. Pictures of Tibetan gods and goddesses. We made a fire of cow manure. It filled the room with foul smoke, but we managed to dry a few things that had gotten wet. We cooked our own supper, out of sympathy for the frightened boys. I made a late meal of parched rice and good American ham and coffee. I will now stretch out in front of the idols, and sleep in peace.

June 2d.

To-day our road lay down the valley of Dongola. There were more traces of cultivation. I saw some stunted pea vines struggling for growth in spite of the altitude. The valley continued for several miles, where it connected with two more forming a kind of "T"; we followed one of them, and went up instead of down. About ten o'clock came to the village of Dongola, where there are a few Tibetan houses. We stopped, and had a meal of tsamba and butter-tea which I quite enjoyed. The tsamba is made of barley which is parched and ground. I also ate some Tibetan cheese, which I liked better than the butter. We changed Ula here, so we had new saddle horses, and a new caravan of animals. The mountainsides now began to be wooded. There was a number of kinds of pine and fir, as well as plum, and a kind of small tree I took to be birch. Many trees were quite large, and had long festoons of moss hanging to them. The streams ran between moss-covered banks and stones. We crossed several small cantilever bridges, quite well built, though crude. A number of small lamaseries were perched high up on the mountainsides. The hillsides showed signs of having been visited once, perhaps by Chinese farmers who were sent in 150 years ago; but because the land wouldn't grow rice, deserted it, leaving it in possession of the Tibetans again. We also saw the remains of several of those interesting Tibetan towers. About 2 P. M. we arrived at a solitary rest-house, just at the foot of the Ga-zhi-lu, a double pass. We decided to stop for the night, as our luggage didn't arrive until five o'clock. There is a full moon, and the view outside is glorious. The silvery light is shed over the mountains and valleys, making them look all the more beautiful in its soft glow. The best room, which we have, is something fierce. The floor is of rough earth, with an ash heap and a pile of stones in the centre where a fire was when we came. Smoke from the adjoining rooms filters through the thin partitions, so that I have been shedding tears while writing this, not tears of sorrow, however ; but because of the pungent fumes from the Tibetan fires. I tore some paper from a window, preferring to risk cold from the draft than endure the smoke. I think I can stand it better asleep. So here goes.

June 3d.

The sun was just kissing the mountain tops and creeping down into the valleys as we started. We were feeling fine after a good night's rest and a good breakfast. A heavy frost made the air crisp and bracing, so we were in splendid spirits for what was in store for us. We had a pretty stiff climb for about 2,500 or 3,000 feet. The mountains began to be more heavily wooded. Saw great pines fifty to sixty feet high as far up as 14,000 feet. As we neared the top the road ascended a steep bank, and we suddenly came out on top of the pass. It was a gentle, undulating surface that met our eyes, with patches of snow here and there. Good grass grew even at this height. A mani mound with flags flying was just beside the road and marked the summit. We got off our horses to let them graze while we turned to view the scene before us. A magnificent range of mountains lay to the east of us. Far below extended valley after valley thousands of feet deep, separated by ridges that were actually mountains. After our view had crossed a dozen or so of these immense valleys, the snow-capped mountains began. The range extended over about one-fourth of the horizon before our view was cut off by nearer mountains. We were about 14,500 feet, and above the snow, while we reckoned the snow a little lower on the mountains which might be called the Frontier range. Great peaks rose above the snow line like immense icebergs. They were sharp, irregular and jagged. The whole horizon was serrated, like great saw teeth. The mountains rose one above another, and seemed piled up in a remarkable way. But far above all rose the majestic peaks that were perfectly dazzling in their grandeur. By careful estimation we decided that they were nearer 30,000 feet than 25,000. There were immense mountains even above the snow line which tallied 14,000 or 15,000 feet. With my glasses I counted one hundred and twenty-five peaks which rose so far above the snow line that we estimated them at 20,000 feet and upwards.

As we ascended the other crest of the pass, we departed from the regular road, and ascended a hill which took us up to an altitude of over 15,000 feet. We quickly dismounted to see the new scene. If the first view was grand this one was marvellous beyond belief. I had no idea that so grand a scene could be found in the world. I wanted to cry out with admiration and praise to God for such beauty. My heart was so filled with emotion that I could scarcely speak, and tears came to my eyes when I saw what God had done. Our field of vision was almost a complete circle. I made a careful estimate of it, and decided that only about sixty degrees of the circle was obscured from view and that only by snowy mountains 15,500 or 18,000 feet high within five miles of us. The rest of the circle, or about three hundred degrees, was clear, and with no obstructions to the wonderful panorama. Our view extended over a radius of two hundred miles, with us in the centre of this wonderful series of mountains. The range we saw was continued to the north and south, for hundreds of miles. To the north the peaks were not so high, yet they were far above the snow line. One great cluster of peaks was even higher than the two to the east of us. We felt it safe to say not far below 30,000 feet, if any at all. We estimated that it rose 15,000 feet above the snow line. It was magnificent indeed, stern, cold, commanding. It was a veritable monarch of the ranges—a peer among the peerless. One interesting thing we noticed. An indistinct haze or mist clustered about the summit of a peak resembling a halo. It seemed to be distinctly not a cloud, but a peculiar vapor, whether caused by hot springs or subterranean fires remains to be discovered.

I made a photo of these mountains, though in order to place my camera I had to rest it on its carrying case, and lie down in the mud to focus it. But it was a rare scene, and one which I fain would preserve. No one who has not had a similar experience can understand what thrills of emotion filled my breast. Here I was drinking in the beauties of a scene which for grandeur and splendor is doubtless unequalled in the world. These mountains undoubtedly rank among the highest on the globe. Here were these great peaks, four or five above 25,000 feet at the most conservative estimate, and a grand sweep of the horizon, extending for at least five hundred miles, with range after range of unnamed mountains and peaks, all above 15,000 feet. Hundreds of them at least 20,000 feet. I feel perfectly sure the scene cannot be equalled anywhere in India on the Tibetan border. Conversations with people who have been there, as well as photographs, convince me that the view cannot compare with this; and not only that, but few people have had the privilege of beholding them from this place. In the first place few white men have visited the region, and in the second place it is very rare indeed that one gets a view so free from clouds; not one marred our view. It is certain that most of the great travellers have not seen it, for some of them spent weeks waiting for them to rise, that they might get a glimpse of these master monarchs. Yet here I was, an insignificant country boy, steeping my very soul in the splendor of the most magnificent scenery on earth. A view which has been denied to all but a very few. I felt that it would be good to build tabernacles and remain here; but time was passing, and the keen wind seeking out the thin places in our clothing, so we led our horses down the steep mountainside, slipping and sliding over the snow and ice, until we came to the regular road below. I can never forget these great mountains. They seem to stand out in my mind even now, and appear to be indelibly fixed among the pictures that hang on memory's wall.

Nor was this all that was to fall to my lot today. We began our descent with the valley that leads to the Yalung River. The road went down, down thousands of feet, until we were about 11,000 feet again. The mountains and valleys were marvellously beautiful. There were virgin forests of pine, fir and oak, many of the pines being one hundred feet high, and the forest so thick that I could see but a few feet from the road in many places. Many of the trees were covered with festoons of moss, lighter in color and finer in texture than the famous Spanish moss (or old man's beard) of our Southern states. Fires and storms have at times devastated the forests. In many places the mountainsides were strewn with a network of fallen trees, scattered like so many straws. The undergrowth was also very rank as we descended, until it became a veritable jungle.

By this time we had gotten into an entirely different climate. The sun shone down with summer heat. The air was warm and balmy, and the gentlest zephyrs stirred. The air has been laden with perfume from countless wild flowers of strange and peculiar beauty; many are entirely unlike any I have ever seen. The flora and fauna in this valley becomes strangely tropical. Parrots are found in the forest. Monkeys are said to live here. Bears, wolves, leopards and other large game are found here in abundance. The peculiar climate of this valley is an interesting thing to the scientists who have had their attention called to it. One other interesting thing was the abundance of wild fruits that we saw growing along the roadside, which was often a pleasant shady lane. We recognized cherries, plums, peaches, possibly quince, or a kind of wild apple. Grapes are said to grow here too, and I saw a peculiar kind of fruit about the size of a black haw which I did not recognize. There were also other berries which doubtless are good for food. The trees were all bearing well. Many had small, green fruit on them. Some in higher altitude were just in bloom. We saw a number of ruined villages, many of which were very old. There were very many culivated fields of wheat, which looked green, and gave promise of a good crop. These were surrounded by a crude fence made of poles, much as we have in timbered sections of the South. We passed the residence of the headman of this district. It is quite a pretentious dwelling.

About 3 : 45 P. M., we came to a picturesque little Tibetan village (Ba kah lea), or octagonal tower, in a very pretty part of the valley. There is a good inn, so we put up for the rest of the day. One of those peculiar towers is here, and said to be one hundred and fifty years old. My belief that they were for religious purposes has been strengthened.

It is poorly situated for defense, almost useless for that. Our animals arrived about 5 P. M., and I enjoyed a good supper, then went for a walk up a small, interesting ravine, which gives evidence of having been a lake at some previous time. This is a wonderfully pretty region, and quite warm and pleasant even at night. We walked back by the light of the full moon. The silvery light flooded the valley with a soft glow, that made even the sharp, stony ridges look beautiful by its magic power. It is a wonderful place, fascinating, picturesque, interesting and altogether lovely. Our room has only a dirt floor, but is not bad, and I have been quite comfortable while writing this. I would gladly write more of what I have seen to-day, but the night wanes, and to-morrow has its journey and duties, demanding strength which must be obtained from "sleep that knits up the ravelled sleeve of care." Let me say that the glorious things of this day have amply repaid me for the unpleasantness of the house-boat trip. The lice, fleas, bedbugs, filthy inns, smoke, bad food, bad beds, and all else, fade into insignificance when I think of the "compensations." Again I render thanks to God the Maker of all this, and to Christ my Master for allowing me the priceless privilege of serving Him in this wonderful part of His footstool.

June 4th.

Not having a hard day before us we slept late, and did not get off until about six o'clock. Though the sun had not reached the valley, it was touching the mountain tops with its brilliant light, making them beautiful indeed. The morning air was delightful and bracing. I was more pleased than ever with the valley. I slept well, and the night was a pleasant one. The valley soon became a gorge, with sides of stone almost beyond possibility of scaling. I think the walls were easily 2,000 to 4,000 feet deep. Vines and flowers, as well as ferns, were plentiful. I saw some yellow violets which I stopped to pick. We were completely shaded at times by great trees of pine and oak and boxwood. Often the road was a narrow cut in the side of the cliff, far above the stream. The horse as usual persisted in trying to see how close to the edge he could walk without falling off. About ten o'clock we came in sight of the muddy waters of the Yalung River. This was a brisk, rapid stream, a good deal further across than man could cast a stone. On the east bank is a group of Tibetan houses, which constitute Ho Keo. We found an inn after some delay.

After dinner we went out to see what could be seen. The village itself is not very interesting. The streets are quite filthy, and inhabited by calves, hogs, chickens, fierce dogs and children; all of which play together quite freely. If one of the animals is pushed out of the way by some one to make room for the baby, the animal seems quite grieved. We looked in at the temple of the city god, which contained a few dilapidated idols, with their mouths smeared with opium. The river attracted our attention next, and we saw there a skin boat or coracle. A fellow was rapidly and skillfully crossing the river in it, and I at once wanted a ride. It was something new, and I wanted to try it. The coracle is made of rawhide or undressed skins of yak, stretched tightly over a willow framework, and is oval-shaped, like a giant oyster shell. It is about three feet wide and five feet long, by fifteen or eighteen inches deep. It weighs about eighty catties, and so can easily be carried overland. As I stepped in the soft skin it gave beneath me, so that it was most unsteady footing. We seated ourselves on the bottom, while our steersman got on his knees, and with a short paddle, pushed off and rowed up stream a short distance, then rapidly crossed the swift current to the other side. When ready to return we asked him to shoot a small rapid just below the ferry for us. At first he objected, but the promise of some cash won his consent to be pushed out. The little boat was caught by the rapid water and tossed like an egg-shell. Our steersman warned us to sit still or we would get wet. There is little danger of being upset, but one feels rather unsafe to say the best of it. The boat was so light it was caught by the current and carried down like a leaf. We were tossed about from side to side, and held on to the framework to keep from bouncing out. Sometimes water splashed in upon us. We shot like an arrow through the rapids, and in a short time our skillful boatman landed us safely on the bank with only a bit of water on our clothing. I enjoyed it immensely, and would have ridden further down, but the man did not like to carry the coracle back so far. Anyhow, I had the new and thrilling experience of riding in a skin boat, and of shooting a rapid in it. The inn where we are staying is peculiar in one sense, that it has a large crop of vermin, about five times as voracious as any I have been in yet. The cracks in the walls are literally filled with their eggs and larva. Bedbugs, fleas and lice are much in evidence, and some have been bold enough to attack me while writing. The walls are jet black, but not with paint. The smoke of years has deposited its soot on the rough boards. Still the room is light, and not altogether bad. The moonlight is lovely on the mountains and river, and I would gladly take a stroll outside, but something tells me I had better stop and go "Hunting."

IX

At the Top of the World

June 5th.

NOT having a very strenuous day before us we slept late, and took our time with breakfast. By this time carriers came to take our things to the ferry. Everything was put on a large, clumsy boat, and we started across the river; the boat went through a pretty rough rapid, and dipped a lot of water. Really it seemed more dangerous than the coracle. Horses and yak were on hand for our luggage, and we had a most deafening jamboree for an hour or so getting loaded and started; so that it was somewhat of a relief when I felt the saddle beneath me again, and we were on our way. The air was balmy, and perfume laden from the many flowers and trees. We saw parrots flying about. At midday we stopped by a stream for lunch, made a camp-fire and boiled some tea. I feasted on Boston baked beans, English jam, Chinese bread, and home-made cookies. It was a regular festal meal on the rocks.

June 6th.

Our drivers had us awake at 4:15 this morning, and in a short time we were up and had breakfast. We then started up the valley that is said to be so often frequented by robbers. However we saw nothing of them and went on our way peacefully. The road led persistently up grade, and we often had to stop to let the horses rest. The sky was nearly covered with great banks of white clouds, which in the distance blended so perfectly with the snow-covered mountain tops that it was hard to tell where the one ended and the other began. After a couple of hours' steady climbing we reached the top of the pass Ramala, something over 15,999 feet. Behind me was a great snow-capped range of mountains rearing lofty peaks, a hundred miles away. I counted forty near the 20,000 mark. A number of deep patches of snow were scattered about, one of which furnished me a large lump to quench my thirst. The road now ran around the side of the mountain, making a gradual descent into a deep valley. Then we ascended as high or higher than the first crest, and turning the road again descended 1,000 feet or more, and up to a third crest as high as the others. Our road now lay for a few miles along a gentle undulating table-land, about 14,000 feet above sea level. Suddenly the road turned down the mountainside, and I saw almost beneath me the flat mud roof of a Tibetan house. We stopped and tied our horses, and took a look around.

The place is called Bolonzugi. I was told that it was the home of the "highest official" in China, being at an altitude of about 14,500 feet. This official is stationed here for the purpose of extirpating the robbers, but judging from appearances he has had a hard time to keep from being extirpated himself. The hut was a most miserable one. The walls on one side of the den were built of sod, on the other of stone. The walls in no place were more than ten feet high, and in some places one could easily step from the ground to the roof of the house. The roof was a mud one, supported by poles, and having one or two openings in it to allow the escape of smoke and entrance of light. The house was almost entirely surrounded by heaps of manure much higher than itself. This harbored a swarm of flies and other insects, and emitted a foul odor. We went within to have a look. One half was evidently used for a stable. The house was dark, and the stench almost unbearable. I carefully picked my way through the filth to get a glimpse of the interior. In the far corner was a room sometimes given to travellers who are unfortunate enough to have to spend the night here. On the opposite side was a dirty, smoky Chinese kitchen. The filth was indescribable. Two beings more like fiends than humans crouched on the floor. One was a woman strong and vigorous, in middle life, but dressed in the dirtiest, coarsest rags imaginable. Her hands and face appeared to be entire strangers to water. The other appeared to be a man, very old. He had closely-cropped hair and blue eyes. His face was dirty almost beyond belief, his clothes of filthly, coarse rags. The whole scene and inmates were most disgusting, both to sight and smell. We tried to bribe them to let me take their pictures, but without success. While waiting for our caravan we took a walk, hoping to find some water I could conscientiously drink. I found a boggy, wet place free alike to hogs, calves, horses and yak to wade and wallow in. This was where the water came from we were to use in making our tea. By this time our things had arrived, and we spread a dirty saddle blanket on the ground in front of the house and had lunch in spite of the filthy surroundings. About two o'clock we came to the official rest-house in Shignolah, and put up for the day.

There are a number of strictly Tibetan houses, and the people are quite picturesque in dress and appearance. Several dirty old men got up and kotowed to us as we went in, looking very much like Indian chiefs. The women have a very peculiar way of dressing the hair. It is braided into numerous small braids, about the size of a lead pencil, which hang to the waist. In front is a cropped lock that falls to the end of the nose. On the head is worn a peculiar head-dress, composed of strips of black cloth about two inches wide, fastened together by silver discs, one of which hangs down over the back of the head, and the other two over the ears. The discs are about three inches in diameter, made of silver, and variously ornamented with coral or beaten figures. Two of these are placed on the sides of the head, just a little above the parietal eminences,

Gewhji, near Samba

Dr. Loftis in the Coracle

while the posterior one is a little above the occipital protuberance. The ribbon-like bands fall down below the waist, and are united by long strings of bright colored beads; some are glass, red, coral, turquoise, jade, shell and a peculiar brown wooden bead. There are also chains of silver and mother-of-pearl at various intervals in the dress. We tried to photograph some of them, but the women ran like scared rabbits as soon as I appeared with a camera. The offer of cash had no effect. Finally I focussed my camera the best I could for a certain distance, then walked unconcernedly about with it under my arm until they got used to it, then made a snap-shot of a woman at a loom weaving, while another sat on the ground with her back to us. The women also smear their faces with butter, which gathers dirt, and helps make them more hideous. Naturally the Litang women are about the ugliest Tibetans there are, and use all the artificial means they can to increase their ugliness, or rather hide their beauty, a thing which seems to me to be altogether superfluous.

We are stopping in the usual official inn. Though we are at about 12,000 feet, it is quite pleasant and comfortable. We must change Ula here, and the chances are we will be late getting off to-morrow. I was much interested in a little table-land about 10,000 feet above the city. It has an area of about ten square miles and a little lake on it. There was splendid grass, and a large number of cattle grazing. From the opposite mountain I made out with my glasses the ruins of two small villages apparently entirely deserted. The hill-sides leading up to the table-land are steep and rough, so that it is accessible only in a few places.

May 7th.

It was about 2:30 when we finally got away with our miscellaneous caravan. We had horses, large and small, a mule and a donkey, as well as some yak and a steer. We soon left the beautiful little valley, and ascended the side of a mountain which was quite well timbered. The climb was not difficult, and we were soon on top of the pass which is about 14,000 feet. There was some fine grazing land. This was a kind of table-land we had come upon, and we travelled along for some time over the gentle undulating ground. Then the road veered a little to the south, and descended into a valley well wooded, and with a large mountain stream flowing through it. There was evidence of a fair population. On the way down we saw an old woman gathering sprouting grubs. The animal or plant was about one and one-half inches long, slightly yellow, and resembled a caterpillar. From the posterior end grew a brown sprout, two or three inches long. They are highly prized as an article of diet, and are quite expensive.

Shortly after descending into the valley we stopped for dinner, where there was a Tibetan house built of small logs, much after the plan of log houses at home, except the roof was the usual flat, dirt roof. After quite a rest we started up a peculiar, long ravine that finally led to the top of another pass. Once on top we were at an altitude of about 15,000 feet. Again we were on a great rolling plateau of grass lands. I saw hundreds of head of yak grazing. The grass was quite plentiful, and of good quality. We travelled quite a while on this plateau, getting magnificent views of many valleys, with just enough timber to break the monotony, and give some shade to the cattle from the heat. The sun's rays are very powerful on these mountains, and soon blister. We made a gradual descent into a pretty valley, where there were a number of black tents of the nomads, and hundreds of yak and sheep grazing.

My horse was fagged out, and I had to drop behind the others. We had not gone far up the mountainside until it was very clear my horse could not go. He had to rest every few steps, and seemed worn out. I then got off to walk and lead him. We were a long way from the top, which is practically 16,000 feet. The higher we went the more fagged the horse was, and I had to stop every ten or twenty feet with him; not only was the horse tired, but I, too, often had to sit down to rest. I felt no effect of the altitude except that every few steps made me gasp for breath, and caused my heart to pump vigorously. But still I kept on. All the others soon left me, with the exception of a soldier, who rode behind and drove the horse, while I walked and tried to drag him along. The road seemed terribly long, and the pass awfully high, but I succeeded at length in reaching the summit.

The sun had been shining vigorously, but now a strong cold wind swept over the mountain top. I paused for a few moments to rest and admire the scenery. Though the clouds shut off some of the mountains, I was able to get a magnificent view of the great snow-covered range which lay to our south several days ago. (I counted eight peaks I felt sure must be 25,000 feet.) It was a lovely sight, and I could not help but admire it, even though I was so exhausted. The road now led around the side of the mountain, making a gradual descent. I struggled against the wind, and led my horse for some distance. Then I saw that the road finally descended into a valley 200 feet below me, and that an old path formerly descended at once into the valley to follow the mountain stream. I then left the travelled road and struck off down the steep path where perhaps white men's feet had not trodden before. It was a very steep and tiresome descent, but I reached the bottom at last. After resting a little, and quenching my thirst with some snow water, I mounted the pony again. He seemed quite refreshed, but plodded along slowly. Once or twice I saw a number of the rare yellow poppies, and stopped and gathered a few, and stored them in my hat. This, with the wind, made it very difficult to keep my hat in place. Still we plodded wearily on. I was tired and uncomfortable, and it had gotten quite cold, and the stiff breeze which came up the valley seemed to penetrate to the bones. At last I saw a rest-house before me. I welcomed it, and managed to alight, and found the others had been here some time.

This place is called Ho-chu-ka. A river runs not far below us, called the Ho-chu River. A strange name. Ho is Chinese for river—Chu is the Tibetan word which means river, while the English word gives it the name the third time. It certainly is well named "river." It has been a strenuous day; we crossed three large mountains, while I had to climb a 16,000 foot pass, and almost drag a horse over. A good night's rest will be welcome.

June 8th.

The official from the place went with us to act as our escort to Litang. He was a nice fellow, and we got quite friendly with him. We followed up the Ho-chu River for about twenty or thirty li, and stopped at a rest-house for dinner. While there we saw three Chinamen on their way out from Batang. They had been sent in as colonists, and tiring of the hardships of the place, decided to make their way out. They were hungry, without money, sick and walking with heavy loads. We felt sorry for them, and gave them some eggs, Tibetan butter and two rupees. The poor fellows almost bumped their heads off on the ground kotowing to us. They were subject to arrest, but we spoke to the official and soldier with us, so that they were unmolested. However we later learned that they had received four hundred stripes at Litang, and ordered to return. This is a very shameful way the officials have of treating the colonists, and would not be tolerated in a civilized country.

Our road now turned up a ravine which led to the next pass. The mountain is about 15,000 feet but does not seem so high. The usual grassy slopes with many cattle met the eye, with here and there the black tents of the nomads. As we neared the top we saw a huge bird, resembling an eagle, flying along. We dismounted, and I made my way up a small gully with my rifle. Though a stiff wind was blowing broadside I took aim and fired. The bird was dead when I reached it. Its wings measured 100 inches from tip to tip, and its head nine inches in diameter. I cut off the head as a trophy of my first kill on the Tibetan border. We now began to descend, and soon came in sight of the Litang plain. It is between mountains 15,000 and 17,000 feet and is itself at an altitude of 14,000 feet. The plain is triangular in shape, roughly speaking, the river running along the longer side of the angle. It is approximately one hundred li long, thirty or forty li wide at its greatest width, with the other two sides about sixty li in length. It is a beautiful undulating plain, growing more smooth towards the river, which runs at the base of high, rocky, snowy mountains. It is for the most part a sandy plain. As we rode across I noticed the soil very closely. The basis of it seemed to be the same as the tops of the passes we had just crossed—vertical or oblique strata of shale and slate, and a kind of soapstone, and more or less a kind of yellowish white clay. On top of this was a stratum of sand, gravel and small stones, with a bit of soil in it. This was more than ten feet deep in many places, occasionally deeper. The stones are worn, as by the action of water, and are of various kinds, quartz, granite, sandstone, flint, limestone, etc. Distinct layers seem to show that they were deposited by water. On top of this is often found a layer of pure sand a foot or two deep, having been apparently blown up in the ridges. Then on top of this is a layer of soil (stratified) resembling the Loess soil. It is free from stones in general, and evidently deposited by winds.

As one ascends higher these strata gradually give way to the regular rocky soil of the mountains. There is a deep gorge at the lower end of the plain, through which the river flows. All the evidence seems to point that this has been a great lake, and that it at last broke through the gorge, leaving this deposit of sand, stones, etc. Winds and rains have done the rest. In the summer this plain is green with grass, and covered with thousands of head of yak, horses and sheep, etc. In the northern angle of the triangle, which is the obtuse, is situated the city of Litang. This city is unique in many ways. It is most likely the highest city in the world. It is also one of the dirtiest. It possesses one of the largest lamaseries outside of Lassa. We reached the city about 1 P. M., and at once went in search of an inn. The official sent his man to see if we could be accommodated in the lamasery. This was a delightful prospect, and we feared it was too good to be materialized. However, soon the man returned saying that a place had been secured. We were then escorted into the "forbidden city," for such the lamasery is, and taken to our rooms.

X

Lodging in the "Forbidden City"

THE building in which we are quartered is of stone and mud, joined in among many others of similar appearance. The lower floor is dark, damp and foul, but the one above is quite agreeable. The large room in front has two small windows, a board floor, plastered or cement walls, and a ceiling made of poles five or six inches in diameter. The interior was decorated with dozens of the most grotesque paintings, which really are not without artistic merit. Several large posts which help support the floor above were decorated with colored scenes. The pictures are of Buddha, elephants, Chinamen, etc., etc. A storeroom and kitchen furnish our suite of rooms. Just across the hall is a large room which is the holy place where the idols are. It is locked. This also is rich in mural decorations. A stairway, or ladder, leads to the flat roof, from which we can get a splendid view of the Holy City. A remarkable thing this, our being lodged in the lamasery. A few years ago it would have cost a man his life to visit the city, and much later it would have been death to have tried to enter, or even exhibit too much curiosity about it. Doubtless we are the first foreigners ever to be lodged in this holy monastery. The clever official realized that it was not the safest place possible, and had two soldiers with guns guarding the door, to see that no harm came to us; a soldier also accompanies us about the city. After getting as comfortably settled as possible, we went for a walk through the lamasery. We met with no resistance, and visited the courtyards of many temples. After lunch we went out for a stroll through the city of Litang proper; we found it arranged somewhat in the form of a circle, or ring, hollowed in the centre with the rude houses scattered about. First there is the lamasery, then the business section, which is half Chinese and half Tibetan, and then the strictly Tibetan portion. It began to rain, but we kept on in spite of it and the fierce Tibetan dogs which threatened to devour us. Though we are 14,000 feet it is not cold, and we felt little effect of the altitude—only tired quite easily. It was nearly dark when we returned after a walk of two or three miles, and we had seen much of this picturesque and interesting place.

June 9th.

Our quarters are in the centre of the Holy City, which is composed wholly of temples and residences of the lamas. There were two large buildings with domes made of copper, plated with gold. The largest measured thirty by fifteen feet. In addition to these were ten or twelve large spires on each roof, six or eight feet high, and two feet in diameter. The plating was of heavy, beaten copper, covered with a layer of gold about one-sixth of an inch in thickness. The buildings are of stone and mud, forming a kind of cement, which is very tenacious. Most are square or rectangular, two or three stories high, and jumbled together without regard to order or convenience of streets. From every roof flutter many mani flags, and various ornaments. There are many great barrel-shaped things, resembling a skirt of coarse yak hair, hung from hoops. I was unable to obtain its religious significance. The smoke was still rising from the morning sacrifices, sent up from many housetops. The hum of lamas repeating the prayers, and the ringing of bells used in worship, broke the stillness of the morning. I made several photos from the roof, half expecting the lamas to set up a vigorous protest, but was not molested.

We sent our cards to the official, asking for an escort through the temples. An interpreter soon came, and accompanied us about the buildings. We learned that we really were the first foreigners to be allowed to take up our quarters in the sacred city, and that only lately had the Chinese been permitted to stay within. We first went to the large temple where the abbot lives. We entered a massive gate, and found ourselves in a great courtyard in front of the main building. It is a massive, stone affair, with great golden roof and spires. There is a large portico in front, with great wooden pillars, and large curtains of yak hair suspended from above. The walls of this porch were painted with idols, the wheel of life, Buddha and many things pertaining to Buddhism. The ceiling had once been covered with silken tapestries, which now hung in threads and rags, the building being about five hundred years old, but in a good state of preservation. The massive door was well barred, and braced with great plates of iron, and hinges and hoops of the same metal. This was crudely but beautifully inlaid with gold, and gorgeous colors, and gold leaf liberally used. At our guide's command the door was opened, and we stepped within the Holy Temple, perhaps the first foreigners that had ever stepped within. The scene before us was strange, yet wonderful indeed. The only light that came in was from the door which was left open, and the great dome above. The corners of the room were as dark almost as a cave. At first sight the room seemed a great forest of draped pillars. By counting I found there were eighty—ten rows one way and eight the other. They measured about fifteen feet apart, and were twelve to eighteen inches in diameter. This made the size of the room about 140x180 feet. The posts under the dome were about thirty feet high, the others fifteen or eighteen feet in height. These posts were nearly square, and covered with long silken, woolen and linen draperies. They had been of many bright hues, but time and dust had reduced them to rags in many cases. Many scrolls were hanging, made of silk or fine linen, and painted with the pictures of various idols, and symbols of

Buddhism. Some were five by six feet wide, and ten to twelve feet long. Across the width of the room on either side of the posts ran rows of cushions, twenty in all, some two feet square, made of coarse material. On these sat lamas muttering prayers, counting beads, and turning small, hand prayer-wheels. All of three walls and part of the fourth were covered with great paintings, well done, in bright lasting colors; but many were obscene, and would not be allowed to enter the United States ordinarily. Only by the light of matches and candles could we see them at all. On the side opposite the door were numerous idols of different sizes and kinds. Many were gilded, and had silken robes thrown about them. There were brass and copper vessels used for burning cedar bushes, as well as many butter lamps. We spent much time in this room observing, taking measurements and writing notes.

Two flights of stairs took us out upon the roof among the spires and domes of the building. Here we got a most magnificent view of the city of Litang, and I did not wonder that this spot was chosen by the abbot as his headquarters, and that he had built his great temple here. We were now led around through one or two dark rooms and halls to a dirty black curtain, hanging in front of a door. This was raised, and we were ushered into a dark room, where there was a solitary lama sitting on a divan. It was hardly necessary for us to be told that this was the great abbot of Litang. His excellency rose to greet us, and received us quite cordially, but with the dignity one might expect from such a man. After much exchanging of polite bows we were seated before him, though he himself did not descend from his couch. The only light which entered came through small windows behind the abbot, so it was difficult to see his face until accustomed to the light. We found him to be a fleshy man, of about two hundred and twenty-five pounds. He was thirty-eight years old (in this present existence). He had closely cropped hair, and a fat round face. His nose and mouth large, his skin brown, or copper-colored. He seemed to be a jovial, good-natured fellow, and laughed softly with us several times during the visit. He spoke in a low, pleasant voice, and only Tibetan, and was not a specimen that would cause one to rave over the "cultured lamas." He wore a heavy robe of dark red, coarse, woollen cloth, thrown around his body, leaving the right arm bare. In his hand he held a string of wooden beads, which he ran through his fingers constantly. Before him was a low table, on which were several large, brass pots, and other vessels of earthenware. Buttered tea was quickly produced, and for a time we sat drinking and talking with the abbot under his great golden roof. We got some interesting information from him, concerning some rare and sacred Tibetan books. One, the Kang-gyur, is here. The blocks for printing it are kept in this monastery. Formerly the Tan-gyur was here, but had been removed to Derge.

There is a story that it took seventy mules to carry the blocks. The first blocks are about three hundred years old, and when the book is printed it comprises 3,700 lamas, who have been ordained in Lassa, and who, including the attachés of the temples and students who came here to study, number, it is said, at times 10,000, occupying the Holy City.

Our stay permitted us to take stray glimpses around the room. Near him, on his left, were a few shelves with glass fronts, enclosing idols. We feel sure we are the first white men received by his holiness. A vase of artificial paper roses stood near by. The sides of the room were covered with scrolls, tapestries, paintings and idols. Not caring to tire his excellency, we remained only ten or twelve minutes. We bowed ourselves out of his august presence at last, very much elated at the success which had fallen to us this day, in not only entering the sacred buildings but in meeting the abbot himself. We now went through a very interesting room, in which were a number of odd and curious things; guns, swords, spears, teapots, etc., etc. It would have been a paradise for a lover of curiosities. A visit was now paid the kitchen of the lamas. There were a number of immense vessels here, but what interested me most were four huge, brass kettles, built into the stone furnace after the fashion of a Chinese stove. After measurement they were found to be eighty inches in diameter, and about thirty-six inches deep, by one inch in thickness, used for preparing food for the

3,700 lamas. We went outside through Litang, and climbed a small hill, where we could get a good view of both the sacred city and the business section which adjoins it.

This part of town is a kind of double triangle with the bases together. The upper half is occupied by the lamasery, and is surrounded by a wall of stone and mud, not very substantial to be sure, but still one which it was not safe for unbelievers to try to pass a few years ago. In the other portion, the houses are so closely joined together that it is hard to distinguish one from the other. The streets are merely passageways, in many places about three feet wide. One can walk over most of the city on the housetops. We then went off down into the plain to the strictly Tibetan section. There are two large buildings, which were formally the residences of tusas or kings. The thing that lured us off down there was a house where a Grand Lama had been born. We finally found it, a dirty, tumble-down place, much like the usual Tibetan house. It was two or three hundred years ago when this great man was born. Four others of smaller rank found birth here also, as is indicated by great wooden blocks like dumb-bells which were suspended over the door. The size varies, showing that all were not of the same rank. The down-stairs room is used as a stable, is dark and filthy, and had a cow in it at the time of our visit. The Dalai Lama was born in this room. We climbed up a flight of rickety stairs to the next floor, which is now used as a kind of lamasery. One room seemed to be a roosting place for chickens. A frisky, young dog kept up such a noise barking, we could scarcely think. We were now shown into a small, dark, dirty den where there were a lot of filthy idols and dusty books, mostly covered with nasty old draperies. The sunlight never enters, and had I not had a candle, I could not have seen a thing. The ugly old woman in charge wore huge silver plates, about eight inches in diameter, on the sides of her head. Our guide could give us no information. He was careful to explain that the lamas, who had lived some hundred years ago, had died before he was born, and that he did not know them personally.

June 10th.

All through the night I heard the constant drip of water from the long spouts leading from the flat roof. I was aroused by water leaking from the ceiling on my bed, and had to get up and move it. When we arose we found that it had been snowing also. It was still falling softly, but with the exception of the battlements of the temples, the roofs were free from it, as it melted as fast as it fell. We could not go on, so I sent my card to the official again, asking for an escort to the place where the sacred Kang-gyur is printed.

In a short time we started out through the mud and rain, and soon found ourselves in the courtyard of a dilapidated old temple. The yard was covered with manure, and large, foul pools stood in the centre, made of water percolating through the manure. In a small side room some lamas were printing pages from the great wooden blocks. They regarded us with disfavor, but after some delay they yielded to the command of our escort, and unlocked the great doors, which as usual were iron-barred, inlaid with silver. The room into which we were shown looked like a great library. It was one hundred and eighty by sixty feet and twelve feet to the ceiling. Running across the room were ten rows of shelves, forty-two feet long, and ten feet high. The blocks were arranged in these shelves on their edges. Each row was divided into eleven sections of nine tiers each, making ninety-nine shelves to each case or row. Each shelf of the ninety-nine contained thirty-five to forty-five of the wooden blocks. As there are ten of the cases, it meant nine hundred and ninety shelves, and as there are about forty or more blocks to each shelf there are likely forty thousand blocks. Each block is made from a single slab of wood, average size twenty-eight by twelve by three-fourths inches. Each one is engraved with the raised Tibetan characters on both sides, and a border about one-fourth inch wide around the edge. The work is fairly well done, though roughly carved, the letters raised from three-eighths to one-half inches above the board. By weighing a board of the same size we found it to weigh about three catties. Based on this calculation the 40,000 blocks would weigh

120,000 catties or 160,000 English pounds. The paper is made near Doaba, a lamasery to the south of Litang, and it takes thirty men three months to produce one copy of the book. The blocks are colored a dark red by the ink used for printing. The abbot himself told us these blocks were about three hundred years old.

The lamas in charge here were the most uncivil and unfriendly we had yet met, and would give us but little information. They were not at all pleased to see us measuring and counting, and making notes of what we saw. A number of the printed pages were spread out on the floor to dry. The paper was rough, coarse, slightly brown, with uneven edges. Each sheet was twenty-seven by nine inches and printed on both sides. Some few had pictures of Buddha, but most were only the Tibetan characters. Each page had the lines running lengthwise, eight lines twenty-two inches long to each page. The characters were one-half inch high. The pages are bound into a volume simply by laying them between two large wooden boards which serve as a cover to the whole, and then tied with a strip of rawhide. The Kang-gyur comprises one hundred and eight volumes, which is one of the sacred numbers of Buddhism. Each volume is about twenty-eight by eight by eight or twelve inches, the boards forming the back being one to two inches thick and often elaborately carved. Sometimes the edges of the pages are cut smooth, and colored, or decorated, with Tibetan symbols.

The possession of these blocks is one of the things which makes the Litang lamasery famous.

After some hesitation and much delay we were permitted to go up-stairs. We entered through another massive door into a room that was so dark my candle scarcely was able to dispel the gloom sufficient to enable us to walk without stumbling. In front was an immense Buddha in a sitting posture, and about ten feet high. All but the face was made of copper, heavily plated with gold. It sat on a great throne of the same material, while behind it was an elaborate background of beaten copper and gold. The idol was draped in fine silk-like veiling, vari-colored; a golden crown was on its head. There were numbers of smaller idols, and many sacred books half hidden among the ancient hangings, but so darkened with age and dirt as to make it almost impossible to tell of what material or color they had originally been. We now climbed out on the roof and proceeded to measure it. We found it to be thirty feet long, seventeen feet wide and ten feet from the eaves to the comb. This was surmounted by three large spires which were six or seven feet high, and two or three feet in diameter. The ends of the roof were gabled, and each of the four corners were decorated with great, golden dragon heads very fierce looking. The roof is made of large sheets of copper riveted together, and plated heavily with gold. This is the roof under which the abbot lives.

Kanger Building

Principal Hall of the Litang Monastery

We now descended to the gallery surrounding the great room in the temple, and there saw an interesting sight. Seated on a throne near the centre of the room was the abbot himself, dressed in his flowing robes. Seated thus he was supposed to be Buddha, and was worshipped as such. Seated around him on the cushions amid the pillars were hundreds of lamas. All were sitting cross-legged, as Buddha was in the habit of doing. We took up our stand in the rear, unobserved, and watched the peculiar performance. There was the hum of the priests as they chanted the prayers, then the slow, dignified clashing of cymbals, following the lead of their great lama. From darkened corners came the blare of trumpets at regular intervals. The scene was most weird, and caused the cold shivers to chase one another up and down my spine. As I watched I realized its significance, and knew they were worshipping this fat, lazy lama as a god! We had watched the strange proceeding for several minutes when some of them espied us among the shadows above. The trumpets ceased, the cymbals came to a standstill, while an ominous silence reigned and all eyes were turned in the direction of the foreign infidels who had dared enter this sacred place, and watch the holy ceremony. We lost no time in beating a hasty retreat. For a moment a great hoarse cry arose from the throats of the lamas inside, then all was quiet, and we knew that worship was resumed. But I cannot forget that scene, and the sickening feeling that crept about my heart as I watched it. We returned to our room where the soldier still kept guard. It was time to rest a while, and get ready for the start to-morrow.

XI

The Journey from Litang

June 11th.

THE morning dawned fair, and we began to get busy to leave Litang. The mountains looked very pretty in the morning sun, their summits showing clear and distinct above a layer of clouds. Our Ula came and we got the things started. We then went to the telegraph office to send a telegram to the friends at Batang. My horse was a very good animal, but extremely skittish, and I had to watch him carefully to prevent trouble. In the meantime a frisky young yak got on a stampede, and strewed our bedding about the plain, before it was finally recovered, and against his protest, made known by much grunting, was resaddled and reloaded and led on again. Once fairly started our road lay across the plain and over some low-lying hills, and a little valley strewn with great limestone rocks. Here were some hot springs, and crude bath-houses had been built for the use of the lamas of a near-by lamasery. We were in need of a bath, so dismounted and went in. The little huts were of stone and cement, while a small bath-tub had been built in the ground with pieces of timber. The lime salts in the water had deposited on the wood, petrifying it, so that it was virtually a nice smooth bath-tub of solid stone. The water was so hot I had to get used to it by degrees. We enjoyed the "soak" for some time, and then proceeded on our journey. The road now ran across a long stretch of the plain which was almost swampy. A small stream ran across it, in which I saw many small minnows, while at the river near by I saw baited hooks for fishing, indicating that there are fish even at the altitude of 14,000 feet.

After lunch we crossed the river and started up from the plain. The plain this side is of strange composition. At one place were immense deposits of stone about the size of a man's head. They were of flint, limestone and granite, chiefly, and worn smooth, but not rounded like those found in river beds. They appeared to have been ground together as in a mill. Where the stones had remained in contact rubbing together were little, cup-like depressions, more or less covering the stones, very shallow but quite distinct. We decided this must have been the moraines of a glacier. These rocks were scattered over quite an area, and were often in heaps and ridges many feet deep. There were also many stones which seemed to be clearly of volcanic origin, having been thrown up by some upheaval in times past. After crossing the river we entered upon a most interesting region. It was a long, gentle slope, strewn with large granite boulders. It was spread out fan-like at the bottom, gradually blending with the plain. It was at least miles wide at its base, but higher up it seemed to narrow to about one mile between high mountains. There could be no other plausible explanation of this than that it was the path of a great glacier. The boulders are strewn about without regard to kinds of stone, or lines of cleavage. They vary in size from that of a football to the size of a cottage dwelling. Their edges are not sharp and distinct, as they would be if they had been thrown directly to the plain from above or below. But they were worn smooth, somewhat resembling the rounded pebbles in a stream. In many places they were piled together in great heaps and nearly covered with earth. The bed of the stream was made entirely of them. Some of the larger ones were widely scattered over the grassy plain. It was impossible for them to have rolled down from the mountainsides. They are not steep enough, and too far away. The road continues to follow up this moraine. Rocks with distinct striæ were plentiful.

As my horse showed a tendency to wander off up the hillside instead of keeping the road, and as he seemed to have a little surplus energy, I let him go. So I went up on the side of a long ridge which ran parallel to the road. This ridge, which was four or five hundred feet above the road, seemed to be made up entirely of boulders and soil brought there by the glacier. One peculiar thing was that there were great streams of water running just beneath the surface in many places. Sometimes they came out of the ground, ran along ten feet or so, and then sank again. I could look down between piles of stones and see the water flowing along. Being some distance from the road I found it nearer to cross a pass than to return to the main line again. So I ascended to the top, which I'm sure was not far from 16,000 feet. As this was not on the road, I doubt if other foreigners have crossed it before me. From there I caught my last glimpse of the glittering spires of the golden-roofed lamasery, some eighteen miles away. Strange to say I found the same kind of granite boulders on top of the pass. I now had to pick my way down the rock-strewn mountainside. At last I had to walk and lead my horse. However, I soon joined the road, and overtook the caravan which had stopped at a solitary rest-house in the valley.

We unloaded and prepared to spend the night. The glacier that cut this valley must have been a gigantic one, and hundreds if not thousands of feet deep. Judging by the rocks so high up on the mountainsides I am of the opinion that this glacier has been intimately connected with the formation of the Litang plain. It seems that originally what is now the plain was a large basin with a bottom of oblique or vertical strata of shale, slate or clay. The outlet below may or may not have been closed at first, but probably was. The big glacier pushed its way down into the basin, and as the ice melted a lake was formed by the dammed up water. The melting ice deposited its soil and rock, at first far out in the basin, then nearer the edges it gradually ceased to exist. A valley at the upper end of the plain suggests the possibility of another glacier. Through this last valley flows the Li River which in times past has been a much larger stream, and has assisted in bringing down material into the basin. On the north side of the valley are some peculiar ridges, which very much resemble sand dunes. As the ice melted the column of water was possibly so great as to finally burst through the gorge below, almost draining the lake. A bare sand plain was then left, and as the prevailing winds are from the south, the sand on the northern side was blown up on the hills, and gradually covered with soil and grass. As a large part of the plain is marshy, it seems quite probable that until a few years ago part of the plain was covered with a lake. The bed rock, or primary soil, is mostly shale, slate, clay, etc. The area near the springs was of limestone, and evidently formed partly by volcanic action. The mountains to the south and west seemed mostly of granite. This will some time make an interesting geological study, but I can make only a few unscientific observations.

While out walking we saw a number of Tibetans, hunting the peculiar grass insect which I mentioned the other day. It is the "Sprouting Grub." The men seek a grassy, level spot, and stoop down looking for the brownish sprout which protrudes above the earth. Their practiced eyes enable them to see one very quickly. Each man is armed with a small, iron pick. When he spies a sprout he rushes forward with a shout, and buries his pick in the earth near it, and soon digs it up. I hunted for a long time before I finally was able to see any at all, and at last came away with four. The sprout springs from the centre of the head, and the root seems to fill the entire body of the worm. The insect is evidently some kind of a caterpillar, and from one to two inches long. The sprout is juicy, but the grub when cut is about the consistency of a sweet potato. These sprouts, worm and all, form a dish which the native and Chinese prize very highly. Three hundred grubs bring one rupee, or about twenty-five cents.

I was busy writing when the servants came rushing in and excitedly announced that there were two great yellow birds outside. I hastily got my rifle and went out and saw what seemed to be two yellow ducks. The wind was blowing hard, and my shot only seemed to make them fly across the stream to return again in a short time to see what was going on. Guns were new things to them. This time I was more successful and killed one. It was about the size of the ordinary tame duck. Its body was yellow, shading into spotted black near the tail with black tail feathers ; its head a lighter yellow, with black beak and one or two black bands around the neck; the wings pure white beneath. On top near the body the feathers are small, soft and white; these shade into yellow at the fore edge, a few short, gray feathers at the other edge, next to these white feathers in the middle section are a lot of long feathers, of a shining dark green color. The large feathers forming the tip are black. As we have been living on salt meat the last ten days this fresh bird was quite a welcome treat.

June 12th.

At Totang long before day our drivers were up wanting to start. It seems that the men are unable to sleep well here in this altitude (about 15,000 feet), and are only too anxious to get up and start. At last we got off after my horse had a spell of pitching and running. The valley was the same boulder stream valley as before, while the mountainsides were unusually rough and rocky from glacial action. This pass is over 16,000 feet, and is called the "Huang tu gong" or Desert Ridge. On top of the plateau were a few small lakes, one directly on the top and the other a short distance down. For a number of miles it was the wildest and most weird looking place I had ever seen. On all sides were these great rocks, and barren peaks. They were too rough to hold much snow. It was cold, and the wind whistled keenly across the pass. Even though I had on heavy clothing I got quite cold. The whole area seemed to be the dumping ground of nature after she had finished making the earth. It seemed as if all the material not wanted in making the mountains, etc., had been deposited here, without reference to order or appearance. Until recently it is said to have been robber infested. This seems to be its only practical use. A body of soldiers was stationed here all the time to exterminate the robbers.

The road gradually descended for some miles into a little valley, through which a stream was flowing in a northerly direction (all others have run south so far). This steep slope seems to be the terminus of a glacier. It is several hundred feet deep, and seems to be made up entirely of glacial débris. The apparent path of the glacier is four or five miles in some places. From the Li River, which is the western end of the moraine, to the top of the pass is forty or fifty li; from here to the eastern extremity about thirty or forty li. It seems as if this pass had been the dividing point of the glacier, and that the débris had been worn down from near here. If so there must have originally been a range here 30,000 to 35,000 feet in height! Altogether it was a terrible pass, and one which you must come to dread more and more the oftener you cross it. After lunch we descended into a road which runs into the Lamaya Valley. We found pines and cedars again, the first trees we had met with since leaving Shingola. As we descended the valley it became more beautiful, and the vegetation more luxuriant. Various tree shrubs and wild flowers made it look most beautiful after the dreary pass. It was also quite hot—a sharp change after the bitter cold.

Towards evening we came to the little village of Lamaya. It is situated on the right banks of the stream, between hills which look bleak and barren, though grassy. Here we saw the first cultivated land since leaving Litang, a pleasant thing to see again. As we came near the village we saw a magnificent range of mountains ahead to the north-west. They are the roughest and shortest peaked we had seen, and must range from 18,000 to 25,000 feet, as best I can estimate. Mount Gehnyi is at the southern end of the range. We stopped in a Tibetan house, built of mud and stones, and two or three stories high. The first floor is used as a stable, and was full of animals. Our room is just above. The walls are of mud and full of vermin. Every now and then a bug drops down, or else knocks off part of the mud ceiling on us. There is a single small hole in the roof through which light and air enter. The room is innocent of chairs and tables. I am seated in a kind of bench made by placing a door on some leather bags of rice, and have my two suit cases arranged as a table. My only light is a flickering candle. Such is the place where I pass the night. The altitude is near 13,000 feet.

June 13th.

We enjoyed a late sleep, as our Ula had not arrived. The little mud hole was not altogether uncomfortable, and we felt quite refreshed. The road ran up quite a steep ravine which was of clay and shale and slate. The land was treeless, and shaded off into grassy knolls above. Evidently some great glacier had made its way down the valley. There are a number of distinct ridges of stone or earth across it from one side to the other, with the exception of where the stream flows through. There are six of them at quite regular intervals, and fairly uniform in appearance. It seems as if this had been the remains of the glacier ; each ridge being where the glacier had reached and melted during the summer. Another thing is a large area of hot, gassy springs. Some have built up a base of solid rock several feet high, and bubble out on top of this. Another interesting thing is the large number of mani mounds. I counted 217 from four to twelve feet high. They were pyramidal, arranged in a row, extending along the road which ran obliquely across the valley. The body of each was made of sod, while there was a layer of finely carved mani stones on the outside. The land is not cultivated here, and it is said there is some cause or command of the lamas that it must not be used. Still it is 12,000 feet high.

Having left the beaten road we had some difficulty in getting down to the main line again, where runs the Rati River. We now followed up the stream, and we passed a large drove of Tibetan snow cock, but the soldier was somewhere else with my gun. We soon stopped at the rest-house which is the end of the stage for that day. We were thoroughly tired and hungry. I am of the opinion that the traveller in a high altitude should eat often and lightly. He seems to get quite faint if he goes long past the usual time, or even until the usual time, without food. This rest-house is situated a few li from the magnificent Mount Gehnyi. It has snow above 17,000 feet. In one place is a great glacier, apparently several hundred feet deep, and extending some distance back up the mountain. I could see great crevices in the ice with my glasses. It had a greenish color where it had broken and melted off. The whole valley gives many evidences of glacial formation. This peak is a wonderfully magnificent one. It stands out almost alone like a great sentinel. The sides in many places are quite steep, but there seems to be plenty of places where one could make an ascent if he cared to brave the dangers of the snow, ice and altitude.

A mountain storm swept down the mountain while we were eating, filling the air with dust, and lowering the temperature several degrees. We went out for a walk, and I took my gun along hoping to get some more fresh meat. I saw only some rabbits and pigeons, after an extended trip through the woods and underbrush. About dark as I was coming back, at the foot of a great cliff of slate limestone, and a peculiar gray marble, an antelope sprang out of the brush up the mountainside. A rifle shot caused it to hobble on a few steps and stop, while I tried again and found my gun empty. When I had recovered from my surprise the animal was gone. Somebody, evidently the soldier who had been carrying the gun, had removed the cartridges leaving me four or five less than I thought I had. To say I was discomfited would be putting it mildly. I returned and reloaded and went back to the gorge, but it was too dark to see or attempt to follow it up the steep cliff. So I lost my meat after all.

June 14th.

As we started we saw a deserting soldier who had been captured, and preparations were being made to torture him, before taking him to Litang where his ears will be pierced with arrows, and he, perhaps, beheaded. The clouds lay low, and several showers struck us. Once I caught sight of the end of a glacier, quite low down the mountain. It looked like a huge cliff of white limestone, and I could hardly believe it was ice. It looked to be nearly 1,000 feet thick, and is about half-way between our starting point and where we stop for the night, Sanba. We saw 142 more big black tents of the nomads on the plains, with many cattle and yak grazing. There are no trees to be seen near and the region might be called a "yelping wilderness."

The village of Sanba consists of a half dozen sod Tibetan houses, surrounded by manure piles higher than they are. Though the altitude is over 14,000 feet there is an attempt at cultivating a few small garden plots with indifferent success. Across the valley opposite is a huge snow-covered mountain, which appears to be 22,000 feet. It has the biggest deposit of snow and ice that I have yet seen.

XII

A Lonely Grave

June 14th.

NEAR the little stream a short distance below the miserable huts is a solitary grave. It bears the single inscription on the marble slab: "William Soutter, missionary to the Tibetans, died November, 1898." This is also repeated in Chinese and Tibetan. The grave is built up with sod and stones, three or four feet high. The grave looks pathetic in its loneliness, and in this dreary wilderness. It tells the final chapter of a life given to the Master's cause in Tibet. In company with another he was taken sick with fever while en route from Batang. They stopped in a miserable, dirty, filthy, gloomy Tibetan house where his life at last ebbed out. I visited the house, and am not surprised that a sick man died there. The lone companion buried his friend as best he could, and went on his way. I could not help feeling a sense of loneliness and sadness come over me as I stood by this lonely grave. It is one of the outposts of the conquering army of our Master, and marks the resting place of one of His pioneers. All honor to those who perish in attempting to clear the way that others may follow them, to lay the foundation for others to build upon. I cannot help thinking of the lonely grave at the edge of the plain. Ordinarily such things do not have any effect on me, but this I must confess causes chilly sensations to creep over me. It is in a most wild, weird, dreary spot. The lofty, snowy Gehnyi stands as a great sentinel over it. Then there is the desolate valley below; on this side, the barren, rocky hills. In the distance are great, flinty, cruel mountains.

It is three days' hard travel to Batang, and four to Litang, across great, awe-inspiring passes. The regions between those places are almost unpopulated, and great wastes of land between. The little stream, passing a few feet away, keeps up a mournful dirge, while the wind sighs across the plains and among the rocks, like the wailing of a lonely spirit. The wild-eyed yak graze near by, snorting and grunting when they suddenly see the white stone. The harsh barking of fierce Tibetan dogs breaks the stillness, and at times yelping of a wolf comes across the plain. The lonely eagle soars far above, while occasionally the hoarse croak of a crow is heard. The wandering nomad pitches his tent near by while the wild Tibetan herdsman rushes by on his shaggy pony. Many months sometimes pass before a white man stops at the sight of the grave, and if he does not actually take off his hat, he feels like it. The sight of this solitary grave causes a man to pause and reflect that this too is more than likely to be his lot, if he remains long in this part of the country. But I'm glad to remember that though the grave is a lonely

Mr. Soutter's Grave at Samba

Headman at Samba

one, the soul of him who sleeps there is not lonely. He doubtless enjoys the companionship of the choicest spirits, and needs not to be pitied. Still his grave stands as a great landmark in a heathen land, as a mute testimonial to the statement that "greater love hath no man than this." May thy bones rest in peace, O servant of God, and may your lonely grave inspire those who follow you to fight harder, and with clenched teeth enter the conflict to remain to the end. O my Master, if it is Thy will that I fill a lonely grave in this land, may it be one that will be a landmark, and an inspiration to others, and may I go to do it willingly, if it is Thy will.

XIII

Above the Clouds

June 15th.

OUR Ula horses were fairly good, but the yak were the wildest creatures we had had, quite in keeping with the place. As we neared the top of Sanba pass we were enveloped in fogs and clouds. It is over 16,000 feet, quite cool, and snow scattered up and down the pass for some distance. Passing an immense mani mound on top, we started down the steep slope, so steep I had to walk and lead my horse. When we had finally descended into the valley we stopped for dinner and to enjoy the view. This is the great Da So valley. The scenery is said to be some of the finest in the world. On all sides rise great limestone mountains, many thousands of feet high, the sides, almost vertical, forming a kind of canyon. They rise in some places fully 4,000 feet above the valley, and to an altitude of 18,000 feet or more. In some places great bluffs rise almost perpendicular for half this distance. The sides in most places are not smooth, but jagged, rocky, and rough almost beyond description. Great ravines are in the hillsides, and great caves yawn at the travellers far below in the valley. The tops of the cliffs terminated in great peaks, barren and rough, which often rose hundreds of feet above the rest of the mountains. Sometimes great forests clung to the mountainsides for a thousand feet or more, and they were absolutely bare the rest of the way, not a blade of grass, or a drop of snow or water to be seen. The cliffs were often vari-colored, and again were of blue or turquoise color looking like a stone set in a green setting. Some places they were light enough to be mistaken for snow or ice at a distance. A rushing river, the Da So, ran through the valley, blending its music with that of the birds.

It was truly a fairy scene in some respects, but grand and sublime. I have never seen anything to equal it. The Yangste gorges were as nothing. In one place I saw a gorge in the mountain, 3,000 feet above us, which would have been equal to any of those on the Yangste, and then had room to spare. We were 3,000 feet below, and then 14,000 feet above the sea level. We stopped for lunch, and a fire was made in the open, and after an hour our yak came. Two or three had evidently run away, upsetting things terribly, while one gave an exhibition of what he could do by running through a lot of brush with some bedding, tearing it badly, while we could only look on and smile (?).

After we had ridden about two hours we crossed the river, and up a small slope, keeping all the while a sharp lookout for the friends who were to meet us. Suddenly I saw two black figures ahead with white hats. I gave a shout, and urged my pony on. They saw us, too, and then there was a puff of smoke, a report from a rifle, and then another as a salute to us. I hurried on and dismounted, met the two men, and when we had made ourselves known, found them to be Mr. Muir of the China Inland Mission who came to meet Mr. Edgar, and Mr. Ogden of our mission who came to meet me.

It was a simple but joyful meeting for us two, after we had been anticipating it for two years or so. We came up to the inn and had tea, then later Mr. Ogden and I went for a walk until dark, and have been putting in the time talking. This is a beautifully mild place. A valley such as one may dream of, and read about for a lifetime, and never see it or its equal. I could not have picked out a more picturesque valley on the road. I am more than glad to have the privilege of enjoying a few hours in this beautiful spot. I am delighted to see friends again, even though they are strangers in a way, yet we have planned and thought of this day for many long months, even years, and now that it is about to be consummated it is hard to realize it. To-morrow we hope to cross the last high pass, and then be in the Batang Valley where a long, steep descent will carry us at last into the city of Batang, the goal I have aimed for so long.

June 16th.

After a long, steady climb we reached the top of the Da So pass. It is said to be over 17,000 feet. Though our horses went slowly, and rested often, they showed no special difficulty in crossing the mountain. Great limestone peaks rose much higher than the pass, giving the place a most desolate look. It was pretty cold up there, and a small lake near the top had ice on it. It was doubtless easily several hundred feet higher than any we had yet crossed. Down, down we went among pine and oak forests, thousands of feet down, so that when we finally stopped for the night we were about 6,000 feet or more below the summit. The road ran around steep bluffs and startling precipices, and through great forests of moss-covered trees. We all walked down the steep hillside about thirty li farther, to a Tibetan inn near a hot spring. It is warmer here than any place since leaving Ta chien lu, and is about 10,000 feet, I suppose. We brought our beds up on the housetop, under a kind of shed, and made preparations to be comfortable. We are about thirty li from Batang, and to-morrow shall reach the end of my long journey. I took a bath, and washed off some of the dirt and accumulations of the trip. This gave me a chance to put on lighter and more decent clothing for the triumphal entry to-morrow.

XIV

Batang at Last

June 17th.

We practically slept in the clouds, and towards morning I had to cover myself with a rubber sheet to keep out the damp. We slept late, and while eating breakfast Dr. Shelton arrived to give me a welcome. After some delay we made the start, and rode down the valley together. The road was steep, and ran continually down, down. We followed the stream along the edge of the high precipice, and through great forests. The scenery was beautiful, though it lacked the snowy mountains. Shortly we came in sight of the city, situated in the valley below. It is a bunch of mud houses, irregularly thrown together. This then was the place I had been heading for so long. Soon we caught sight of Dr. Shelton's two little girls, Dorris and Dorothy, who had come to meet me on their donkeys, and I was glad enough to see them. We then rode on down alongside fields of wheat and barley, entered the city, and rode down the slippery, stony street.

We rode to Dr. Shelton's house where I met Mrs. Shelton, who gave me such a royal welcome as would almost repay one for the long trip. After a few minutes, we went to Mr. Ogden's house, and met his wife, a charming little woman who gave me a most cordial welcome. Everybody went to Dr. Shelton's for dinner, and we had a most excellent time. To say it was a treat to me was to express it mildly. It was a regular home dinner, the best I have eaten since leaving—well for a long time. It was a treat to be with these good people—Kansans and Kentuckians. They were my people, and I never felt so much at home as I did with them, since coming to China at least. Well, the dinner was great, and I enjoyed every minute of it.

We made a holiday out of the rest of the day, and were about as happy a bunch as you could find even in the homeland, and it was hard to realize that I was so far from "anywhere." It had taken a month and a half to reach Nankin from home. There I was unavoidably detained for nearly five months, and after making the start from Nankin I was four months (minus one day) of actual travelling to Batang. Even then I made a remarkably quick trip from Nankin, so every one says, as I reached here nearly a month before they thought I would. It was a long, hard journey, but I managed to keep well, and happy and strong through it all, and reached my station without serious accident or trouble. I had no difficulty with the altitudes, eating and sleeping without discomfort. I feel I did not do this in my own strength, but that He who said, "Go and I will be with you always" was with me, and strengthened and protected me. To Him I give the praise and thanks.

After a bit I came over to my apartments to unpack a little. I have two splendid rooms in the same building with the dispensary and the chapel, a study and a bedroom. They are clean, light, and well ventilated, on the second floor, overlooking a roaring mountain stream that rushes noisily by. I am now installed in a mud house, with the task of getting two languages and a dialect as the next proposition. The stable and hog-pens are below my room, and at night I am lulled to sleep by the tinkle of the bells on the mules and horses, and by the roar of the stream a few feet away. But I'm very thankful for being here, and hope that in some way I may bring some light into the darkened lives of these poor people here, whom our Saviour died to save. I am highly pleased with the rooms, and think I shall be quite satisfied here. Dr. Shelton and Mr. Ogden quite thoughtfully had some furniture made, and the rooms papered. The good women had put towels, chairs, rugs, a cot, and a vase of flowers on a table, a most pleasing touch given to it all by their hand.

It is hard to realize that my long journey is over. To-morrow is four months since leaving Nankin. I have had a most strenuous trip, and rapidly, too. I have crossed China and part of Tibet. I have crossed some exceedingly great passes and seen some of the most wonderful scenery in the world. I have passed dangerous rapids on frail boats, and done several strenuous stunts. Through it all the good Master has protected me, and I give Him

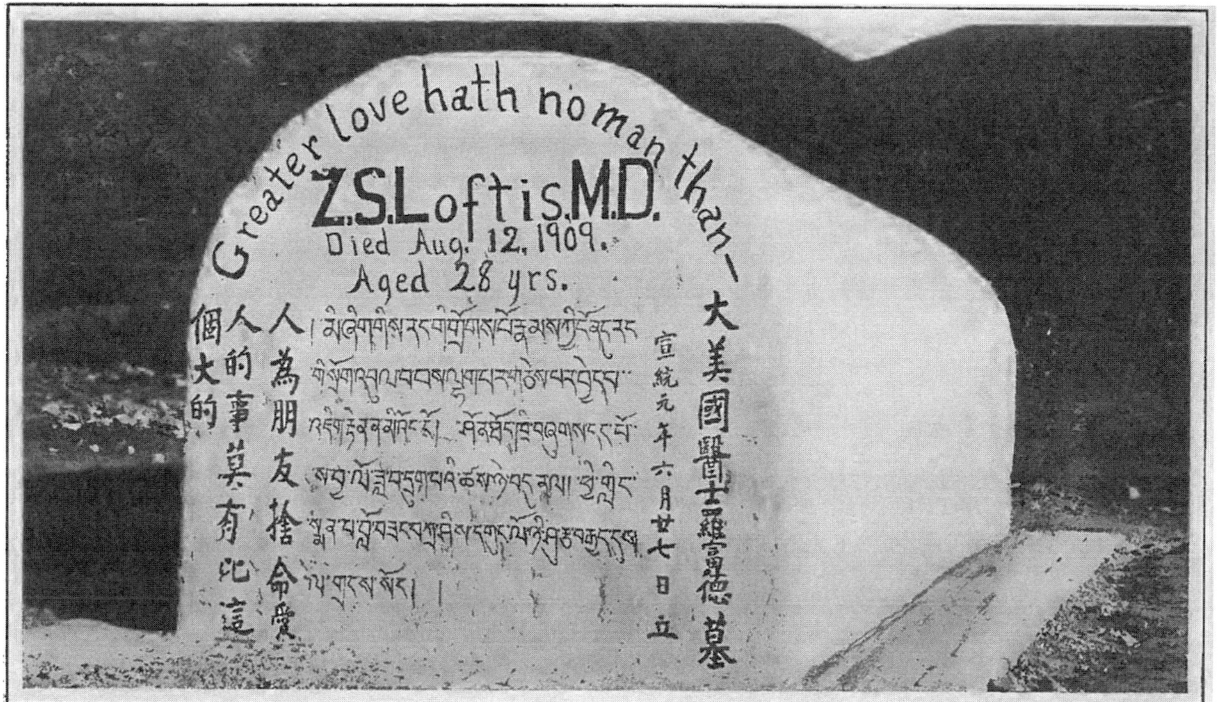

The Grave of Dr. Loftis, Batang

thanks, and owe it all to Him. He has answered my prayers, in a marvellous way, to reach the field of my choice, and now that I am here I hope to prove worthy of His love and blessing. I give Him thanks and credit for it all, and want Him to use my life here as He sees best for the advancement of His cause in this needy part of the earth.

June 18th.

Only in Batang one day! A fellow might have a right to a "gone" feeling, after getting out here. But the sun shines, the grass is green, friends are true, and God is overhead; so all is well. After breakfast we took a look around the brick kiln, where the doctor is burning his brick preparatory to building by and by. We all went to Mr. Ogden's for dinner, an unusually good one, which made me feel quite at home again. I am more and more pleased with the place and the prospects. I am very thankful for being here, and would not exchange mission stations with any living man. Had I selected my own co-workers I could not have been better pleased. I met to-day one of the ambassadors from Nepaul to China. He is on his way back from Pekin, having been some two years on the road going and coming. He gave us a lot of information about Nepaul and invited me to visit him there, saying he would have the Maharajah give me a permit to enter, and send elephants to meet me, twelve ordinary stages from the railroad—three official stages. He lives at Gorkha. He told us about tiger hunting on elephants in cages. He says that Europeans are more welcome in Lassa than the Chinese, and that the Tibetans would be glad to throw off their yoke and fight the Chinese. He will take fifty-two days to Lassa from here, and thirty-three from there to Nepaul. He is of high rank at home, very near the Maharajah. I have been but little in my "home" to-day, but now I am here with the stream roaring outside and the tinkle of a donkey bell somewhere in the distance. It is cool and pleasant, and everything lovely and the goose hangs high.

June 19th.

Slept so soundly had to be wakened for breakfast. Then we went for a ride down to the ruins of the old monastery. It is only a mass of ruined mud walls. It must have been an immense thing in its glory before it fell into the hands of the Chinese. (The outside walls enclose nine acres.) The great courtyard is now being used as a drilling ground for soldiers, about 1,200 being here now.

June 20th.

We all had a pleasant service together. The Lord's supper was observed in the usual way, and it was a spiritual uplift to meet thus together. After services the Ogden family came to the Sheltons', and we all had another splendid meal together. The afternoon was spent in singing familiar hymns, in which we all took part and enjoyed very much.

June 21st.

Have been developing photos to-day, and have some very interesting pictures. It has been a pleasant day, and I feel quite at home in my new surroundings. To-day is a great feast day with the Tibetans. So Mrs. Shelton's Tibetan woman invited us out to see them a while. We went across the river to a tent among many, half hidden among the trees and bushes. There were six Tibetan women, dressed in their holiday clothes. Their hair hung down their backs in long black braids, tipped at the end with tassels of silk and gold. They wore gowns, the necks of which were profusely decorated with red, blue, green and yellow bands. The waist was usually a bright red. They wore long, coarse, blue skirts; aprons of woollen cloth, brown, red and black trimmed with a kind of gold cloth were also worn. Gaily colored, heavy cloth Tibetan boots completed the costume. Long, silver earrings and bracelets were worn in the way of jewelry, also rings and neck clasps. We were seated on rugs and cushions, at a low table about twelve inches high. Buttered tea and parched wheat were brought to us, and we indulged mildly, remembering that microbes do not readily succumb to the temperature obtained by boiling water at this altitude. A leather-headed drum hung in the tent door. A servant beat this and clanged cymbals at the same time, while the women danced for us. It was an odd step, and the hands and body were peculiarly graceful as they kept motion to the time of the music. As it got so hot in the tent we moved to the shade of a few trees where some food was brought us. At last it got too warm, and we left and returned home. Another interesting thing to-day was the visit of the Da Kagi, the chief ambassador to Pekin from Nepaul. This small country was conquered some one hundred and thirty years ago by the Chinese, and now they force them to carry tribute to the emperor every twelve years or so. The journey by sea and rail could be done in a very short time, but the long march across the Chinese dominion is to treat them as captives, impress them with the littleness of their own country, and the vastness of China. The last ambassador made the journey in seven years, and lost one-half of his men on the way. So far only one of his retinue of fifty Nepaulese have died in this the third year. Upon leaving he told us all a friendly good-bye and later sent Dr. Shelton and myself each a Nepaulese pipe, or "Hookah." It is only found in Nepaul. It is of earthenware; the bowl is filled with water, and a long straw connects from this to the smoker's lips. Tobacco is laid on like charcoal in the brazier, and a servant holds the whole thing while you smoke. The pipe bowl is made of a cocoanut beautifully carved, inlaid with silver and pearl. I prize it very highly as a souvenir from Nepaul and a gift from the Da Kagi.

June 23d.

This morning the streets were filled with people watching the procession of Ula and riders of the Da Kagi starting for Lassa. Hundreds of animals bearing loads, with the yellow flag of the Chinese emperor, crossed the bridge and started on the road we are not allowed to travel. Altogether there were 800 animals, 650 for loads and 150 for riding. The whole country has been scoured for Ula, and to-night I miss the stamping and jingling bells from the stable below me. So the Nepaulese ambassador and suite have left, and we have only their gifts.

To-day was the sixth anniversary of Mr. and Mrs. Ogden's wedding day. All the foreigners were invited there for dinner, and had a most delightful time, and everybody thoroughly enjoyed it.

June 24th.

A week in Batang and still getting on fine. Everything quiet. My Tibetan landlady has been on a drunk, and been trying to talk Chinese. A fellow who evidently had an ax to grind came round to-day with a horse which he wanted to give Dr. Shelton to let him join the church. He was told that we didn't do business that way, and he went away sorrowing. One of our patients is a fellow with tuberculosis, who has come twenty-four days' journey for treatment. Poor fellow, I fear he won't get much medicine that can do him any good.

Dr. Shelton and Mr. Ogden and I rode upon the

mountain to-day. The chief object was to find strawberries, or other fruit. We found lots of vines, both strawberries and raspberries, but no fruit, and but little prospect of any ripening. We had not been home long until we were told that a house had fallen down on some Tibetans, killing three and wounding some. Two came to the dispensary bruised badly, and we went to the scene of the wreck to see the other victims. One was a girl of ten or twelve, with bruises on the body and head. We found that a grandmother, mother and child had been killed by the falling walls. These rickety mud houses topple over at the slightest wind or storm.

June 27th.

This morning the little handful of Christians met together in the chapel and sang hymns and praises to our Father. The Ogdens were with us for dinner, and as usual had a nice time together. After supper the courier arrived with the mail, which is the greatest excitement we ever have here.

June 30th.

Spent the morning writing and in the afternoon Dr. Shelton, Mr. Ogden and I went for a ride. After crossing a small pass we came in view of the Yangste, flowing at our feet, the same majestic, muddy stream, though reduced in size. It looks more like the Yangste than anything else; however its banks were precipitous and unscalable, while again it would be spread out over numerous gravel bars and islands. So I made the acquaintance of the mighty river again. For a thousand miles I traversed it on a steamer. For nearly another thousand miles in a house-boat. Then after skipping a thousand miles or more I see it again. Now it extends far up into the great Tibetan plateau, into that wonderful, mysterious country where the white man's foot has never trod. What wonderful mountains and valleys it traverses is only to be guessed at, until some hardy explorer has the strength, time and opportunity to wrest from it its enticing secrets. I returned to my "castle" which the Chinese call "High Fortress." I have just noticed that my house is on the official Lassa road, and that all caravans must pass my door on their way to that mighty city.

July 1st.

Am beginning to take hold of the dispensary work a little more now as Dr. Shelton and Mr. Ogden are going out for a trip soon, leaving all with me. Dysentery is beginning to come in now, so we may expect an early and hard siege of it.

July 4th.

The nation's birthday. However we are a long way from any celebration of it. We had planned a little picnic among ourselves, but a heavy rain during the night put it out of the question. Though our attendance at church was small to-day, it was declared to be the best service we had had in Batang. I enjoyed it very much. I was able for the first time to join in the singing of the Chinese hymns, and after service gave some Sunday-school cards to some children who were there, and managed to explain a little of what they meant.

July 5th.

Dr. Shelton and Mr. Ogden finished preparations for their trip south to-day, and by nine o'clock were off. I went with them out of town a short distance, and then returned to the dispensary to do a little work. I made up a few medicines for stock preparations. Tackled the dispensary alone this morning. Managed to get along very well. Started studying Tibetan to-day.

Was awakened this morning by two Tibetan women knocking at my door. They had a baby with them which I learned was twenty days old. Its mother had been dead some time, and it was almost starved to death. It was little more than a living skeleton, and even then at death's door. It was wrapped in coarse, filthy rags with ashes covering its body, evidently a dusting powder. It has most likely never been washed, at least it did not look it. It was a sight to bring the tears to my eyes. I know what is needed, but could not give it the attention required. I needed a hospital, a place to keep it, and see that it was fed and clothed properly. These things I did not have, and so gave it a dose of medicine and the women some direction which I knew would be disregarded, and turned the poor little thing away to die.

July 12th.

At the close of the clinic this morning a fellow was brought in with a dislocated shoulder. He was in much pain. I gave him an H. M. C. tablet, and in a short time reduced it without pain. They knew nothing about dislocations, and so the thing was something to set them talking and praising the foreign doctor.

July 13th.

Last night I was called to a case of opium suicide. I took my hypodermic and small electric battery, and went. It was a Tibetan who had been drinking and his mother was also drunk. They had raised some kind of a row, and he had taken opium. She was crying when I got there, and he was apparently unconscious. The battery soon caused him to cry "quit." Apomorphine brought out the opium, and when I left him two hours later he was a sicker and sadder man, and doubtless wiser. The old lady did some fancy kotowing to me for my work. This morning the fellow was up, sober and repentant. Another life saved by my being here.

July 16th.

Went out for a walk, and saw some interesting things. Saw a huge boulder pounded full of holes. The holes were apparently fresh, but no one seems to know about them; they are attributed to devils. Found a clay tablet in a Tibetan "pagoda." It is a small votive tablet such as are often seen, but the queer thing was that it was fresh, and perfumed with sandalwood oil.

July 17th.

During the clinic this morning a fellow came in who had been thoroughly spanked. There was a denuded area about five by six inches. The thigh was greatly swollen. He had gotten 1,000 licks on one leg only. My Tibetan teacher told me the Chinese and Tibetans were fighting twelve days from here, in the province of Derge. Eighty lamas killed including the head lama. The lamasery was at Sa Shu, and had over 600 lamas in it; forty Chinese soldiers were also slain.

July 19th.

9:15 P. M. I have just witnessed a rather grewsome sight. To-day a slave woman belonging to my landlady died of syphilis, being nearly rotten. The Tibetan custom is to burn those who can afford it when they die, but the very poor are thrown into the river. Hearing that they were going to dispose of the body to-night, I got on the lookout. As it was raining and very muddy, I put on my rubber boots and storm coat, and watched from the darkness. They waited for some time. I could see several lamas, with the people of the house, sitting in the large room in front of mine. Finally some one evidently of importance came, probably a head priest. Soon after his arrival six or eight men came out in the court or hall between our rooms, and withdrawing a curtain which hung close to the wall, disclosed the nåked body lying on a bed of rags. The lama then filled his mouth with some liquid, and squirted it over the face, neck, and limbs of the corpse. It was then raised to a sitting position, the calves flexed against the thighs, and the thighs against the abdomen, the arms folded and placed in front of the stomach. The head was then forced down, until the brow touched the knees, then a cord was wound around the body several times, using a great deal of force to draw it tight, and hold the corpse in position, much as we would strap a trunk. After the body had been thoroughly tied, it was put in a very small box, such as is used for carrying loads on donkeys. It had no lid. The body was lifted and put in the box, in a sitting position. It was scarcely wide enough for the hips to go in, so they jammed the body down as if it had been so much beef. After it had been pushed, crammed and worked into the box the head and shoulders still protruded above. The lama then took Tsamba and water, and put quite a lot on the back of the neck and head. A coarse, woollen rag was then thrown over it all and tied. One of the men swung the box with its ghastly contents over his shoulder, and lighted by a pine torch, they hurriedly trotted down the stairs and out on the street. During part of the ceremony, "Om Mani Padme Hum" was constantly chanted. I then hurried down the steps just out of sight, and followed the light. They turned down towards the big river which flows below the monastery. I followed in the darkness, not caring to light my lantern, stumbled over rocks, splashed through irrigation ditches, and mud holes, trying to keep in safe range of the light, but not too close. Once I fell into quite deep water, but managed to keep on my feet. They hurried on towards the ruins of the old lamasery, turning to the left of the mani mounds, and the great mass of ruins, instead of going through the central road.

As we neared the river I caught sight of some sneaking, cowardly dogs, worse than curs, that scented the body and were following; they dodged about just in the edge of the circle of light, like phantoms. When the men reached the great mani mound beside the stream, those with the torch went to a hollow tree and stopped, protecting their light. The man with the body, the priest, and one other proceeded to the riverside, and after a few minutes of mani muttering, tossed the box and its contents into the water, and wading out, threw rocks at it until it was caught by the foaming, rushing current, and carried away in the darkness. Yes! the body carried on into a rushing, angry, cold, dark stream, but what a much more terrible cold, dark river of death must the soul have been carried into! As she entered the icy waters, there was no hope of a better land on the other side, such as we know about. She knew little or nothing of the Saviour who beckons to us from across the dark stream. She could not look forward to a happy resurrection with the Saviour, and loved ones who have gone before, as we can do. No tears were shed when her soul departed, nor when her body was consigned to the chilly waters, unless perhaps her two motherless children were old enough to realize something of it, and weep over their loss. O God! let me hope that in some way she received mercy at Thy hands, and that she has learned to know enough of the Saviour to escape the awful death.

As the men finished their last sad rites, I hurriedly retraced my steps to a safe place around the corner of the ruins, lighted my pocket lantern, and made quick time back to my room, arriving some time before they did, who perhaps were entirely ignorant of their observer. After they returned I stepped out of my room, and one of the fellows, who tries to be good-natured, came close enough to me for me to smell his breath, and I knew he had been drinking wine. So this is what takes place in the very house in which I live, and not only that but in the same building where our chapel and dispensary are. The very place where we try to tell of Jesus who died, and where we try to be an example of Him in His teaching and healing. God grant that we may soon bring the light into some of their darkened lives.

As I sit here I cannot help but contrast this funeral with the loving care with which the mother and loved one is put away at home, and how often it is they regard the river of death as only a parting line for a time, and expect to meet on the other side some day. I cannot rid my mind of the thought of the poor, naked body drifting down the rapids and on to cruel rocks, bruised and broken, frightening the fish from their haunts as it rolls along. The box was so frail it never floated half a mile with its burden before it was broken to pieces, and the body thrown out.

I am also reminded of a poor little slave boy who came to the dispensary last Monday or Tuesday. He complained of his back hurting him, said he had been beaten by his master, but there did not seem to be anything serious the matter. Still I cannot forget the appealing look which seemed to mean approaching danger. I called the little fellow back as he went down the steps, and gave him a Sunday-school card. I never saw him again. That was Tuesday; Saturday he was dead; small-pox. He lived just opposite my door. My heavenly Father, can it not be that that picture brought some message to him in his last hours? Some thought that was comforting! O God, help me before it is too late to be instrumental in saving some of these struggling souls who are sinking into a hopeless death, while we are helpless except in Thine own strength.

So ends the diary of Dr. Loftis. He himself left us August 12th with the typhus fever and small-pox. He was trying so hard to care for those poor people. May his words of hope be multiplied a hundredfold, and his death wake up hearts at home, until the ages echo over the loss of this man; gentle, kindly, simple-hearted, earnest and true. How we needed him. How Tibet needed him. For two years we had watched for him, looked for him, and wished for him. It meant another rivet in the stability of the Batang mission. He was so happy to be with us. He was ready as the rest to endure what must come, and what hopes and plans he had, how some day, he as a medical man could go to Lassa, for that day is coming and not many years away, when the great city will be entered by a "Jesus man." Is there a better name than that? He fitted into his work and into our home life beautifully, declaring he would not exchange his life-work with any man living, and declaring in his quiet way, "He had found his folks at last," and we were glad, so glad, to find him. He saved a Tibetan who had taken opium, and the fellow's mother's gratitude was unbounded. He spoke of how glad he was to be so useful at once, and it is only a medical man who can be of immediate use. On Wednesday Dr. Loftis came to breakfast and asked for a little milk toast, said he was feeling badly, went home and to bed. Dr. Shelton said he was in for smallpox or some kind of fever, and went to him and remained until the end. In a day he announced "smallpox"—that was enough. Another day and the unmistakable typhus rash covered his body. Oh, how we hoped and prayed for our little doctor! Did you at home forget him and us? We are very far away from you all. I sent the doctor his meals and did the washing and all I could, but it seemed so very, very little compared with what we and the mission had at stake. Then the afternoon came when I heard Dr. Shelton sobbing in the yard, and he called me, telling that Dr. Loftis had gone. I could not go to him, and he dared not come to us.

It doesn't seem true at all—we have looked so long for him, and feel like this was a dreadful dream and he will still come to us. He had already shouldered his share of the burdens; but now without the hope of his coming and retaking the load, it seems twice as heavy, for we have lost him too. O may his grave cry out to you at home, and as he has said, may it give the inspiration needed to take up his work, and die if need be also even as he did, in obeying the command, "Go ye." His tomb is built on the main road leading to Lassa, a few steps to the side, and all passing may read in English, Tibetan and Chinese.

F. B. S.